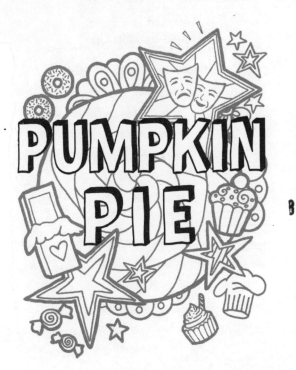

PUMPKIN PIE

B

Also by Jean Ure

PUMPKIN PIE

Jean Ure

Illustrated by Karen Donnelly

HarperCollins *Children's Books*

First published in Great Britain by Collins 2002
This edition published by HarperCollins *Children's Books* 2012

HarperCollins *Children's Books* is a division of HarperCollins*Publishers* Ltd,
77-85 Fulham Palace Road, Hammersmith, London W6 8JB

The aut   e author and

ISBN-13 978-0-00-742484-9

Printed and bound in England by
Clays Ltd, St Ives plc

MIX
Paper from
responsible sources
FSC® C007454

FSC is a non-profit international organisation established to promote the
responsible management of the world's forests. Products carrying the FSC
label are independently certified to assure consumers that they come
from forests that are managed to meet the social, economic and
ecological needs of present and future generations.

Find out more about HarperCollins and the environment at
www.harpercollins.co.uk/green

for all Pumpkins, everywhere

one

THIS IS THE story of a drop-dead gorgeous girl called Pumpkin, who has long blonde hair and a figure to die for. Skinny as a rake, thin as a pin, with long luscious legs right up to her bum.
I wish!

It is my sister Petal who has long luscious legs and a figure to die for. I am Pumpkin, and I am plump. Dad, trying to make me feel better, says that I am cuddly. Some people (trying to make me feel worse) say that I am *fat*. I am not fat! But I did go through a phase of thinking I was and hating myself for it.

I am the middle one of three. There is my sister Petal (drop-dead gorgeous), whose real name is Louise and who is two years older than I am. And then there is Philip, known as Pip, who is two years younger. So you see I really am stuck in the middle. An uncomfortable position! Well, I think it is. Pip, being the youngest, and a boy, is spoilt rotten. (Mum would deny this, but it is true. She is the one who does the spoiling!) Petal, on the other hand, being the oldest, is treated practically as an adult and allowed to do just whatever she wants.

At the time I am writing about, when I got all fussed and bothered thinking I was fat, my sister Petal was fourteen, which may seem a big age when you are only, say, six or seven, but is nowhere near as grown up as she liked to make out. She was still only in Year 9. My Auntie Megan, who is a teacher, says that Year 9s are the pits.

"Think they know everything, and know absolutely nothing!"

Petal was certainly convinced that she knew everything, especially about boys. To hear her talk, you'd think she was the world's authority. She was boy mad.

What do I mean, *was*? She still is! She's worse than ever! I suppose it is hard to avoid it when you are so drop-dead gorgeous. Petal has only to widen her eyes, which are quite wide enough to begin with, and every boy on the block comes running. She ought by rights to be a dumb blonde airhead. I mean if there was any justice in the world, that is what she would be. But it is one of life's great unfairnesses that some people have brains as well as bodies. That's Petal for you. She is not a boffin, like Pip, but she can pass all her exams OK, no trouble at all, without doing so much as a single stroke of work, or so it seems to me. Well, I mean, the amount of socialising she does, she wouldn't have time to do any work. Even in Year 9 she was busy buzzing about all over the place. This is what I'm saying: she's the oldest, so she could get away with it. Nobody ever bothered to check where she was or who she was with.

Actually, I suppose, really and truly, nobody ever bothered to check a whole lot of things about any of us. About Petal and her boyfriends, me and my fatness, Pip and his secret worries. This is probably what comes of having a dad who is (in his words, not mine!) "just a slob", and a mum who is a high flyer.

It was Dad who stayed home to look after us when we were little, while Mum clawed her way up the career ladder. It was what they both wanted. Dad enjoyed being a househusband; Mum enjoyed going out to work. She's into real estate (I always think that sounds more impressive than *estate agent*) and she pushes herself really hard. Some days we hardly used to see her. It was always Dad who sent us off to school and was there for us when we came home at teatime. It was Dad who played with us and read to us and tucked us up in bed. I think he made a good job of it, even though he calls himself a slob. By this he means that he is lazy, and perhaps there may be just a little bit of truth in it. It is certainly true that he always considered it far more important to stop and have a cuddle, or play a game, or go up the park, than to do any housework. But that was OK, because so did we!

Mum used to despair that "the place is a pigsty!" Well, it wasn't very tidy, and the washing-up didn't always get done, and sometimes you could write your name in the dust, but we didn't mind. We looked on it as one big playground. Poor Mum! She really likes everything to be neat and clean. And *ordered*. Dad has other priorities. His one big passion is food. Unfortunately, it is a passion which I share...

Petal is lucky: food leaves her completely cold. She can exist quite happily on a glass of milk and a lettuce leaf. She is a vegetarian and won't eat anything that has a face. Which, according to Petal, even includes humble creatures such as prawns. I know that prawns have whiskers. But *faces*???

"They are alive," says Petal. "They don't want to be eaten any more than you do."

In spite of her obsession with boys – and clothes, and make-up – I suppose she is really quite high-principled.

Pip is just downright picky. Where food is concerned, that is.

He won't eat skin, he won't eat fat, he won't eat eggs if they're runny (he won't eat eggs if they're hard), he won't eat Indian, he won't eat Chinese, he won't eat cheese and he won't eat "anything red". For example, tomatoes, radishes, beetroot. Red peppers. Certain types of cabbage. Actually, *any* type of cabbage. Oh, and he absolutely loathes cauliflower, mushrooms, Brussel sprouts and broccoli. It doesn't really leave very much for him to eat. He is Dad's worst nightmare.

Now, me, I am Dad's dream come true. I would eat anything he put in front of me. And oh, boy! When he was at home, did he ever put a lot! It really pleased him to see me pile into great mounds of spaghetti or macaroni cheese.

11

"That's my girl!" he'd go. "That's my Pumpkin!"

When Pip started school full time, Dad went to work as a chef in a local pizza parlour, *Pizza Romana*, only we all know it as Giorgio's, because Giorgio is the man who owns it. He is a friend of Dad's and that is how Dad got the job. It means he has to work in the evenings, and quite often Mum does, too, so we are frequently left to our own devices. But it doesn't stop Dad trying to pile up my plate! He brings home these enormous great pizzas, which Pip won't eat (on account of the cheese) and Petal just picks at (on account of her sparrow-like appetite) so that I am expected to finish them off. If I don't, Dad is disappointed.

"What's all this?" he would cry, opening the fridge and seeing half a pizza still sitting there. "Come along, Pumpkin! Don't let me down!"

Pumpkin is Dad's pet name for me. Pumpkin, or Pumpkin Pie. My real name is Jenny. Jenny Josephine Penny. Dad calls us his three Ps: Petal, Pip and Pumpkin. I don't know how Petal became Petal; probably because she is so beautiful, like a flower. Pip is short for Pipsqueak. Meaning (I think) something little. Pumpkin, I am afraid to say, rather speaks for itself.

It didn't bother me so much being called Pumpkin when I was little, but it is not such fun when you are twelve years old. It is not dignified. It brings to mind a great round orange thing. Mum says it is a term of

12

endearment and nothing whatsoever to do with great round orange things. Huh! I wonder how she would like it?

At school, thank goodness, I am usually just Jenny, or Jen. Nobody knows that at home I am Pumpkin. Only my best friend, Saffy, and she would never tell. We are hugely loyal to each other. Saffy is the only person in the entire world that I would tell my secrets to, because I know she can be trusted and would never betray me. Needless to say, I would never betray her, either, except maybe under torture, as I am not very brave. If people started pulling out my toenails with red hot pincers, or trying to drown me in buckets of water, I have this horrid feeling that I might perhaps talk. But not otherwise! Like the time in Juniors when she confided to me this big fear she had that she was not normal. She'd heard her mum telling someone how she'd been born in an incubator. Saffy, that is.

"I think I may have developed in a test tube... I could be an alien life form!"

Well, we were only nine; what did we know? Poor Saffy was convinced she was going to start sprouting wings or turning green. Later on, of course, she discovered that she had been born too early and had been *put* in an incubator, so then she stopped worrying about being an alien and got a bit boastful.

"I was a premature baby!"

Like it was something clever. If ever she starts to get above herself I remind her of the time she thought she was an alien, but I have never told a living soul about it and I *never will*. Her secret is safe with me! Because that is how it is with me and Saffy.

Maybe because of being premature, Saffy is incredibly dainty. She is not terribly pretty, as her nose is a bit pointy and her mouth is rather on the small side, but she is very sweet and delicate-looking. She has green eyes, like a cat – she really ought to be called Emerald, not Sapphire! – and feathery red-gold hair. Oh, and she has freckles, which she hates, but which personally I think are really cool. I would like to have freckles! I once tried painting some on but a rather horrible boy in our class yelled "Spotty!" at me, so I didn't do it any more.

Out of all three of us, I'm the one that takes after Dad. Mum is slim and graceful: Dad is *tubby*. He is also a bit thin on top, which I am not! I have fair hair, like Petal – quite thick. But whereas Petal's is thick and *straight*, mine unfortunately is thick and curly. Ugh! I hate curls. I wish I could have straighteners! For some reason, Mum won't let me. There was this one thing I tried, when I spread my hair on the ironing board and ironed it, to get the kinks out, but it just went and frizzed up into a mad mess like a Brillo pad. I didn't try that again! Saffy suggested I should hang heavy weights off it, which seemed like it might work. So I collected up all these big stones from the garden and spent hours in my bedroom sewing little sacks for the stones to go in, I even stitched ribbons on to them – pink, 'cos I wanted them to look nice in case anyone saw me – and I tied them on to my hair and went to bed all clunking and clanking in the hope that I would wake up in the morning with my hair as blissfully straight as Petal's.

Well. Huh! What a brilliant idea *that* turned out to be. First off, I had to sleep on my front with my nose pressed into the pillow, as a result of which I nearly suffocated. Second, every time I moved a stone would go clonk! into my face. Third, I woke up with a headache; and fourth, it had *no effect whatsoever* on my hair. All that hard work and suffering for absolutely nothing!

I should have learnt my lesson. I should have learnt that it is foolish and futile to put yourself through agonies of pain in a vain attempt to be beautiful. But of course I didn't. Saffy says, "Does anyone ever?" I would like to think so. I would like to think you reach a stage where you are content to be just the way you are, without all this stress about freckles and hair and body shape; but somehow, watching Mum put on her make-up every morning, watching her carefully select what clothes to wear (like when she has a client she specially wants to impress) Somehow I doubt it. I feel that we are doomed to hanker after unattainable perfection. Until, in the end, we get old and past it, which surely must be a great comfort?

Although in my plumpness I take after Dad, I think that in many other ways I take after Mum. I am for instance quite ambitious. Far more so than Petal, though not as much as my little boffin brother, who will probably end up as a nuclear physicist or at the very least a brain surgeon. But I wouldn't mind being a high flyer, like Mum – if only I could make up my mind what to fly at. Sometimes I think one thing, sometimes another. Over the years I have been going to be: a tour guide (because I would like to travel); an air hostess (for the same reason); something in the army (ditto); a children's nanny (I would go to America!); or a car mechanic.

It is so difficult to decide. I once tried speaking to Dad about it, because I did think, at the age of twelve, I ought to be making plans. Dad said, "Rubbish! You're far too young to bother your head about that sort of thing. Just take life as it comes, that's my motto."

"But I want to know what to *aim* at," I said.

Dad suggested that maybe I could follow in his footsteps and be a chef. He was all eager for me to start straight away. I know he would like nothing better than to teach me how to cook, but I feel I am already into food quite enough as it is. I don't need encouragement! I've seen Dad in the kitchen. I've seen the way he picks at things. He just can't resist nibbling! Sometimes when he cooks Sunday lunch Mum tells one of us to go and stand over him while he is dishing up.

"Otherwise we'll be lucky if there's anything left!"

She is only partly joking. Dad did once demolish practically a whole plateful of roast potatoes before they could reach the table. He doesn't mean to; he does it without realising. I can understand how it happens, because I would be the same unless I exercised the most enormous willpower. I think food is such a comfort!

I could see that Dad was a bit upset when I showed so little enthusiasm for the idea of becoming a chef. He said, "Don't let me down, Plumpkin! Us foodies have got to stick together."

I thought, *Plumpkin*? I looked at Dad, reproachfully, wondering whether I had heard him right. You couldn't go round calling people Plumpkin! It was like calling them fatty, or baldy, or midget. It wasn't PC. It was insulting!

"Eh? Plumpkin?"

He'd said it again! My own dad!

"It's up to us," said Dad, "to keep the flag flying. Beachballs versus stick insects! There's nothing to be ashamed of, you know, in having a healthy appetite."

Saffy has a healthy appetite. She eats just about anything and everything and never even puts on a gram. Life is very unfair, I sometimes think.

I managed to get Mum by herself one day, for about two seconds, and said, straight out, "Mum, do you think I'm fat?"

She was whizzing to and fro at the time, getting ready for work.

"Fat?" she cried, over her shoulder, as she flew past. "Of course you're not fat!"

"I feel fat," I said.

"Well, you're not," said Mum, snatching up a pile of papers. "Don't be so silly!" She crammed the papers into her briefcase. "I don't want you starting on that," she said.

"But Dad called me Plumpkin," I wailed.

"Oh, poppet!" Mum paused just long enough to give me a quick hug before racing across the room to grab her mobile. "He doesn't mean anything by it! It's just a term of endearment."

"He wouldn't say it to Petal," I said.

"No, well, Petal doesn't eat enough to keep a flea alive. You have more sense – and I love you just the way you are!"

"*Fat*," I muttered.

"Puppy fat. There's nothing wrong with that. You take after your dad – and I love him just the way he is, as well!"

With that she was gone, whirling off in a cloud of scent, briefcase bulging, mobile in her hand. That's my mum! A real high flyer. It is next to impossible to have a proper heart-to-heart with her as she is always in such a mad rush; but it would have been nice to talk just a little bit more.

It was definitely round about then that I started on all my fretting and fussing on the subject of fat.

two

BEFORE GOING ANY further I think I should describe what was a typical day in the Penny household.

Typical Day

8am. In the kitchen. Mum standing by the table, blowing on her nails. (She has just painted them with bright red varnish.) Mum is wearing her smart grey office suit, very chic and pinstriped. She looks like a high-powered business executive.

Petal bursts through the door in her usual mad rush. She is no good at getting up in the morning, probably because she hardly ever goes to bed before midnight.

(As I said before, she is allowed to get away with anything. I wouldn't be!)

Petal looks sensational even in our dire school uniform of grolly green skirt and sweater. The skirt is *pleated*. Yuck yuck yuck! But Petal has customised it; in other words, rolled the waistband over so that the skirt barely covers her bottom. Her tiny bottom. And nobody says a thing! Mum is too busy blowing on her nails and Dad wouldn't notice if we all dressed up in bin bags. But wait till she gets to school and Mrs Jacklin sees her. Then she'll catch it! But not, of course, before all the boys have had a good look...

Mrs Jacklin, by the way, is our head teacher and a real dragon when it comes to dress code. Skirts down to the knee. *No jewellery. No platforms. No fancy hairstyles.* It makes life very difficult for a girl like Petal. It doesn't bother me so much.

I am sitting at the table trying to finish off my maths homework, which I should have done last night only I didn't because I forgot – a thing that seems to happen rather frequently with me and maths homework. I, too, am wearing our dire school uniform but looking nothing like Petal does. For a start, there is just no way I could roll the waistband of my skirt over. I wouldn't be able to do it up! There is a hole in my tights (grolly green, to go with the rest of the foul get-up) and I suddenly see that I have dribbled food down the front of my sweater. From the looks of it, it is sauce from yesterday's spaghetti. Ugh! Why am I so messy?

It is because I take after Dad. He is also messy. We are both slobs!

Make a mental note to change my ways. Do not wish to be a slob for the rest of my life. Begin by going over to the sink and pawing at spaghetti marks with dish cloth. Have to push past Pip to get there. Pip is down on his hands and knees, packing his school bag. He is a compulsive packer. He puts things in and takes them out and puts them back in a different order. Everything has to be *just right*.

Query: at the age of ten, what does he have to pack??? When I was ten I just went off with my fluffy froggy pencil case and my lunch box and my teddy bear mascot. Pip lugs a whole library around with him.

"Don't tread on my things!" he yells, as I cram past him on my way back from the sink.

Pip is wearing *his* school uniform of white shirt and grey trousers. He looks like any other small boy. Perhaps a bit more intense and serious, being such a geek, though I am not sure he is quite the genius that Mum makes him out to be. Although I don't know! He could be. My brother the genius...

What with Pip being so brainy, and Petal being so gorgeous, I sometimes wonder what it leaves for me. Maybe I shall have to cultivate a nice nature – like Dad. Dad never snaps or snarls. He never loses his temper. He's never mean. He's over at the stove right now, all bundled up in his blue woolly dressing gown, fixing a breakfast which only two of us will eat. ie, him and me!

From the way he's stirring it, I would guess that he's doing porridge. Dad's a great one for porridge. He makes it very rich and creamy and serves it up with milk and sugar. Yum yum! I love Dad's porridge. Mum won't eat it because she's in too much of a hurry. She'll just have black coffee. Petal won't eat it because she can't be bothered. She'll probably have a glass of milk and a banana. Pip, needless to say, won't touch it. He says it's all grey and slimy and reminds him of snot. Dad still tries to tempt him. I don't know why he bothers; Pip's a lost cause. Foodwise, that is. All he ever wants is two slices of toast, *lightly browned* with the crusts cut off (he won't eat crusts) and smeared with marge. Butter makes him sick; and marmalade, of course, being orange, is a shade of red and therefore taboo.

Dad and I finish off the porridge between us, sharing the cream from the top of the milk. We're still eating when Mum yells at Pip that it's time to go. She drops him off at school every morning; me and Petal have to take the bus. We don't really mind. It gives Petal the opportunity to show off her legs before Mrs Jacklin gets hold of her, and it gives me the chance to finish off my maths homework. Even, if I'm lucky, to pick someone's brains. Esther McGuffin, for instance, who gets on two stops before us and truly *is* a genius. She is very good-natured and never minds if I copy. The way I see it, it is not proper cheating as I always make sure to copy some of it wrong and have never ever got more than a C+. (On the days I don't copy I mostly get a D.)

At the school gates I meet up with Saffy. We're in Year 7. Bottom of the pile. Petal flashes past us, showing all of her legs, and most of her bum, in a crowd of Year 9s. Year 9s are incredibly arrogant! I can see why Auntie Megan doesn't like them.

On a typical school day, I would say that nothing very much occurs. Of interest, that is. It just jogs on, in the same old way. One time, I remember, a girl in our class, Annie Goldstone, went and fainted in morning assembly and had to be carried out. That caused some excitement. Oh, and another time a boy called Nathan Corrie, also in our class, fell through the roof of the science lab right on top of Mr Gifford, one of our science teachers. Then there was Sophie Sutton, and her nosebleed. She bled buckets! All over her desk, all over the floor. But these sort of events are very few and far between. They don't happen every day, or even, alas, every week. Mostly it is just the daily slog. The best you can hope for is Nathan Corrie being told to leave the room. But that is no big deal!

In spite of all this, me and Saffy do quite like school. We are neither of us specially brilliant at anything, and we are not the type of people to be chosen first for games teams or voted form captain or asked to join the Inner Circle, but we bumble along quite happily in our own way.

The Inner Circle is a gang of four girls, led by Dani Morris, who consider themselves to be the crème de la crème (as Auntie Megan would say). They are the ones who get invited to all the parties. The ones who decide what is in and what is out. Like for instance when they came to school wearing ribbed tights and all the rest of us had to start wearing ribbed tights, 'cos otherwise we would have been just too uncool for words, until

suddenly, without any warning, they went back to ordinary ones again and threw us into confusion.

I personally wouldn't want to be a member of the Inner Circle with the eyes of all the world upon me. I would be too self-conscious!

"We will just be *us*," says Saffy.

Really, what else can you be? It is no use thinking you can turn yourself into someone completely different. I know, because I have tried it. Lots of times! These are just some of the things I have attempted to be:

Bright and breezy, exuding confidence from every pore. "Hey! Wow! Way to go!"

Pathetic. Utterly pathetic.

Loud and laddish. Smutty jokes and long snorty cackles at anything even faintly suggestive.

Total disaster. I boil up like a beetroot even just thinking of it.

Creepy crawly. In other words, humble.

Even worse. I just *oozed* humility. All I can say is *YUCK*.

Eager beaver sports freak. Madly playing football in the playground every break. Dragging myself to school at half-past seven to practise netball in the freezing cold.

Bore bore BORE! I quickly gave up on that one. It wouldn't have worked anyway.

None of them worked. None of these things that I have tried. When I thought I was being bright and breezy, I just came across as obnoxious so that people kept saying things like, "Who do you think you are, all of a sudden?" They don't say that to Dani Morris, and she is just about as obnoxious as can be. But she can get away with it, and I can't!

This is the point that I am making. Like when I went through my oozy phase. All I did was just smile at Kevin Williams and he instantly stretched his lips into this hideous grimace and made his eyes go crossed. Why did he do it??? He wouldn't have done it to Petal! If Petal had smiled at him, he would most likely have gone to jelly. But Kevin Williams is a friend of Nathan Corrie, so I should have known better. Nathan Corrie behaves like something that has just crawled out of the primeval slime.

28

However. To return to this typical day that I am talking about. Here are me and Saffy, sat together in our little cosy corner at the back of the class, and there at the front is Ms Glazer, our maths teacher. She's collecting up our maths homework from yesterday and handing back the stuff we did last week. She's given me a D+. Not bad! I mean, considering I did it all on my own. At least it's better than D-, but Ms Glazer doesn't seem to see it that way. At the bottom, in fierce red ink, she's written: *Jenny, I really would like there to be some improvement during the course of this term.* D+ is an improvement! What's she going on about? I happen to have this mental block, where figures just don't mean anything to me. Sometimes I seriously think that an essential part of my brain is missing. I have tried putting this point of view to Ms Glazer, but all she says in reply is, "Nonsense! There is nothing whatsoever wrong with your brain. Application is what is lacking."

Dad is the only one who ever sympathises with me. Mum, in her ruthless high-flying way, agrees with Ms Glazer.

"Anyone can do anything if they just set their mind to it."

That is RUBBISH. Can a one-legged man run a mile in a minute? I think not! (I wish I had thought to say this to Mum. I'd like to know how she would have wriggled out of *that*.)

To make up for my D+ in maths, I get an A in biology. It's for my drawing of the rabbit's reproductive system. I am rather proud of my rabbit's reproductive system. I have filled in all the organs in different colours – bright reds and greens and purples – so that it looks like one of those modern paintings that make people like Dad go, "Call that art?" I try showing it to Saffy but she takes one look and shrieks, "That's disgusting! Take it away!" She says it makes her feel sick. She says anything to do with reproduction makes her feel sick. She is a very sensitive sort of person.

All through the lesson I keep shooting little glances at my brilliant artwork. It occurs to me that the rabbit's reproductive system, in colour, would make a fascinating and appropriate design for certain types of garment. Those smock things, for instance, that people wear when they are pregnant. It would be a fashion statement!

I get quite excited by this and wonder if perhaps I should go to art school and become a famous clothes designer. Why not? I can do it! Already I have visions of being interviewed on television.

"Jenny Jo Penny, the fashion designer..."

I would put in the Jo, being my middle name, as I think Jenny Penny is just too naff for words. There would be the Jenny Jo Penny collection and all the big Hollywood stars would come to me for their outfits. I would be a designer label! And I wouldn't ever use fur or animal skin. I would be known for not using it.

"Jenny Jo Penny, the animal-friendly fashion designer..."

Hurrah! I've found something to aim at.

But wait! The last lesson of the day is art, with Mr Pickering. We are doing still life, and Mr Pickering has tastefully arranged a few bits of fruit for us to draw. In my new artistic mode I decide that just copying is not very imaginative. I mean if you just want to copy you might as well use a camera. A true artist will *interpret*. So what I do, I ever so slightly alter the shape of things and then splosh on the brightest colours I can find. Blue, orange, purple, like I did with the rabbit stuff. These will be my trademark!

I'm sitting there, waiting for Mr Pickering to come and comment, and feeling distinctly pleased with myself, when Saffy leans over to have a look. She gives this loud squawk and shrieks, "Ugh! It looks like—"

I am not going to say what she thinks it looks like. It is too vulgar. I am surprised that she knows about such things, although she does have two brothers, both older than she is, which perhaps would account for it. All the same, it was quite uncalled for. (Especially as it made me go all hot and red.)

What Mr Pickering says is not so vulgar, but it is certainly what I would call *deflating*. I am not going to repeat it. It makes me instantly droop and give up all ideas about going to art school. It is terrible to have so little confidence! But between them, Saffy and Mr Pickering have utterly demolished me.

Get home from school to find the house empty. Mum and Petal not yet back, Dad has gone off to pick up Pip. Help myself to some cold pasta and slump in front of the television till Dad and Pip arrive. Dad at once bustles out to the kitchen to prepare some food, while Pip settles down to his homework. I hardly had any homework when I was ten, but Pip has stacks of it. This is because he goes to this special school that Mum and Dad *pay* for, and where they are all expected to work like crazy and pass exams so that they can win scholarships to even more special schools and pass more exams and go to university and become nuclear physicists. Or whatever. Me and Petal just used to go up the road to the local Juniors. Nobody cared whether we passed our exams and became nuclear physicists. But Mum says Pip is gifted and it would be a crime not to encourage him. She is probably right. I am not complaining, since I don't seem to be gifted in any way whatsoever. Not even artistically, in spite of getting an A for my rabbit's reproductive system.

At five o'clock Dad goes off to Giorgio's for the evening, leaving a big bowl of macaroni cheese for us to dig into. I help myself to a sizeable dollop and go back to the television. Pip is still doing his homework. Petal comes waltzing in, snatches a mouthful of macaroni cheese and

rushes upstairs to her bedroom, where she spends most of the evening telephoning her friends. Every half hour or so she wafts back down to grab an apple or a glass of milk. I hear her discussing some party that she is going to at the weekend. Her main concern seems to be whether a certain boy is likely to be there, and if so, who will he be there *with*?

"Please not that awful tart from Year 10!"

If it's the awful tart from Year 10, Petal will just *die*. Why, is what I want to know? But it is no use asking her. She has already gone wailing back up the stairs.

"What will I do? What will I do?"

Fascinating stuff! I sometimes think that Petal and I inhabit different worlds.

We all do actually. Me and Petal and Pip. There's Pip obsessed with work, and Petal obsessed with boys, and me very soon to become obsessed with fat. We never talk about our obsessions. We never really talk about anything. We are part of the same family and live under the same roof and I think we all love one another; but we never actually *communicate*.

33

Mum gets in at quarter to nine. She gives me and Pip a quick peck on the cheek – "All right, poppets? Everything OK?" – pours herself a glass of wine and disappears upstairs to soak in the bath. Pip packs up his homework, makes himself a lettuce sandwich and takes himself off to bed. Just like that! Without being told. It doesn't strike me as quite normal, for a ten year old, but that is Pip for you. He has the weight of the world on his shoulders.

Obviously nobody is going to eat Dad's macaroni cheese, so I decide I'd better polish it off to stop Dad from being upset. I then finish off my homework, watch a bit more telly, eat a bag of crisps and go upstairs.

At eleven o'clock Dad comes home from work and calls out to see if anyone's awake and wants a nightcap. I am, and I do! So Dad makes two mugs of foaming hot chocolate and we drink them together, with Dad sitting on the edge of my bed. I love these private moments that I have with Dad! I tell him all about school, about my A for biology and my D+ for maths, and Dad tells me all about Giorgio's, about the customers who've been in and the food that he's cooked. The only thing that slightly spoils it is when he says goodnight. He says, "Night night, Plumpkin! Sleep tight."

He seems to be calling me Plumpkin all the time now. I pull up the duvet and fall asleep, only to dream, for some reason, of whales. Big beached blubbery whales. I wonder what Petal dreams of? Boys, probably.

That was how it was when I was twelve. I'm fourteen now, but nothing very much has changed. Dad still cooks, Mum is still high-powered, Petal still casts her spell over the male population, Pip still does oceans of homework. The only thing is, I no longer dream about whales. That has got to be an improvement!

This is how it came about.

three

IT WAS SAFFY who suggested we should go to acting classes. I was quite surprised as she had never shown any inclination that way. Just the opposite! Once at infant school she was chosen to be an angel in the nativity play, a sweet little red-headed, pointy-nosed angel, all dressed up in a white nightie with a halo on her head and dear little wings sprouting out of her back. Guess what?

She tripped over her nightie, forgot her line – she only had the one – and ran off the stage, blubbing. Oh, dear! It is something she will never manage to live down. She gets quite huffy about it.

"I was *six*," she says, if ever I chance, just casually, to bring it into the conversation. Which I only do if I feel for some reason she needs putting in her place.

When she is in a *really* huffy mood she will waspishly remind me that I didn't get chosen to be anything at all, let alone an angel, which you would have thought I might have done, having fair hair and blue eyes and looking, if I may say so, far more angelic than Saffy. In my opinion, she would have been better cast as a sheep. (Then she wouldn't have had a nightie to trip over, ha ha!)

The only reason I didn't get chosen was that I caught chicken pox. If I hadn't had chicken pox, I bet I'd have been an angel all right! And I bet I wouldn't have tripped over my nightie and forgotten my line, either. Saffy has absolutely no right to crow. It is hardly a person's fault if a person gets struck down by illness.

I have said this to her many times, but all she says in reply is, "You *picked* yourself."

What she means is, I scratched my spots. She says that is why I wasn't chosen.

"It was a nativity play, not a horror show!"

It's true I did make a bit of a mess of myself. Petal,

who had chicken pox at the same time as me, didn't even scrape off one tiny little crust. Even at the age of eight, Petal obviously knew the value of a smooth, unblemished skin. But it is all vanity! What do I care? In any case, as Saffy always hastens to assure me – feeling guilty, no doubt, at her cruel jibe – "It hardly shows at all these days. Honestly! Just one little dent in the middle of your chin... it's really cute!"

Huh! It doesn't alter the fact that she had her chance as an angel and she *muffed* it. It is no use getting ratty with me! What I didn't understand was why she should want to go to acting classes, all of a sudden.

I put this to her, and earnestly Saffy explained it wasn't so much the acting she was interested in, though she reckoned by now she could manage to say the odd line or two without bursting into tears. What it was, she said, was *boys*.

"Ah," I said. "Aha!"

"Precisely," said Saffy.

She giggled, and so did I.

"You think it would be a good way to meet them?"

"I do," said Saffy.

In that case, I was all for it! Meeting boys, in that second term of Year 7, had become very important, not to say crucial. We had to meet boys! There were lots of boys in our class at school, of course, but we had already met them. We met them every day, and we didn't think much of them. Well, I mean! Kevin Williams and Nathan Corrie. Pur-lease! Not that they were all primeval swamp creatures, but even those that hadn't crawled out of the mud seemed to come from distant planets. Trying to suss them out was like trying to fathom the workings of an alien mind. Were they plant life? Or were they animal? They probably thought the same about us. But you have to get to grips with them sooner or later because otherwise, for goodness' sake, the human race would just die out!

I didn't say this to Saffy, knowing her sensitivity on certain subjects. eg, the rabbit's reproductive system. I just agreed with her that meeting boys was an essential part of our education, and one which at the moment was being sadly neglected.

"I don't know how Petal got going," I said. "She just seemed to do it automatically."

Saffy said that Petal was a natural.

"People like you and me have to work at it."

"And you honestly truly think," I said, "that drama school would be a good place to start?"

Saffy said yes, it would be brilliant! She sounded really keen. At drama school, she said, we would meet boys who were creative and sensitive, and gorgeous with it. All the things that the swamp creatures weren't. It's true! You look at a boy like Nathan Corrie and you think, "Is this life as we know it?"

39

The thought of meeting boys who were both creative *and* sensitive *and* gorgeous seemed almost too good to be true.

"Do they really exist?" I said.

"Of course they do!" said Saffy. She said that you had to be all of those things if you wanted to be an actor. You couldn't have actors that were goofy or geeky or just plain boring.

"Or even just plain," I said. And then immediately thought of at least a dozen that were all of those things. I reeled off a list to Saffy.

"What about that one that looks like a frog? That one that was on the other day. And that one that's all drippy, the one in *Scene Stealing*, that you said you couldn't stand. You said it was insulting they ever let him on the screen. And that other one, that Jason person, the one in—"

"Yeah, yeah, yeah!" said Saffy. "But there's far more

who are gorgeous. I mean—" She gave this little nervous trill. Nervous because she knew perfectly well she was being self-indulgent. "Look at Brad!"

By Brad she meant Brad Pitt. (Famous American movie star, in case anyone has been hiding in a hole for the past ten years.) Don't ask me what Brad Pitt had to do with it. Just *don't ask*. Saffy brings Brad Pitt into everything. She can't help it, poor dear, she is infatuated. I somewhat sternly pointed out (being cruel to be kind) that Brad Pitt is not exactly a *boy*, in fact he is probably old enough to be her grandfather. Well, father. I might just as well not have bothered! Saffy simply smiled this soppy smile and loftily informed me that she preferred "the mature man".

"Well, you're not very likely to meet any mature men at drama classes," I said. "Not when they're advertised for 12 to 16 year olds!"

"That's all right," said Saffy, still in these lofty tones. "If I can't have Brad—"

"Which you can't," I said.

"I know I can't!" snapped Saffy. "I just said that, didn't I? He's married!"

"On the other hand," I said, trying to be helpful, "he's bound to get divorced. Movie stars always do. If you wait around long enough—"

"Oh!" She clasped her hands. "Do you think so?" Heavens! She was taking me seriously. Her cheeks had now turned bright pink.

"Well, no," I said. "I don't, actually. By the time you're old enough, he'll be practically decrepit."

Her face fell, and I immediately felt that I had been mean, turning her daydreams into a joke. It's not kind to trample on people's daydreams. Specially not when it's your best friend. But Saffy is actually quite realistic and never stays crushed for long. She is a whole lot tougher than she looks!

"Well, anyway," she said, "as I was saying, if I can't have Brad I'll make do with someone else. Just in the mean time. To practise on."

"While you're waiting," I said.

"Yes." She giggled. "As long as they're not geeky!"

"Or swamp creatures."

"Or aliens."

But they wouldn't be. She promised me! They would be creative and sensitive and hunky. She said we must enrol straight away.

"We've already missed the first two weeks of term. They'll all be taken!"

I said, "Who will?"

"All the gorgeous guys!"

42

"Oh. Right!" An idea suddenly struck me. If all the guys were going to be gorgeous, wouldn't all the girls be gorgeous, too? I had visions of finding myself among a dozen different versions of Petal. What a nightmare!

I put this to Saffy, but she reassured me. She said that loads of quite ordinary-looking girls (such as for instance her and me) fancied themselves as actresses, but the only boys who went to drama classes were the creative, sensitive, and divinely beautiful ones.

"If they're not creative and sensitive they go and play with their computers. And if they are creative and sensitive, but not very beautiful—"

I waited.

"They go and do something else," said Saffy.

"Like what?" I said.

"Oh! I don't know." She waved a hand. Saffy can never be bothered with mere detail. She is quite an impatient sort of person. "Probably go and write poetry, or something."

I thought about the boys in our class. Writing poetry was not an activity I associated with any of them. Ethan Cole had once written a limerick that started "There was a young girl called Jan", but none of it had scanned and it hadn't made any sort of sense and what was more it had been downright rude. That was the only sort of poetry that the boys in our class understood. How could you have a class with *fourteen boys* and every single one an alien?

I said to Saffy that if I could meet a boy that wrote poetry I wouldn't mind if he wasn't beautiful, just the fact that he wrote poetry would be enough, but Saffy told me that that made me sound desperate.

"Why settle for a creative geek when you could have a creative hunk? Ask your mum and dad as soon as you get home. Tell them your entire future is at stake! You don't have to mention boys. Just say that having drama classes will give you poise and – and confidence and – and will be good for your self-esteem."

"All right," I said.

I asked Dad the minute he got back from picking up Pip from school. I followed him round the kitchen as he chopped and sliced and tossed things into pans.

"Dad," I said.

"Yes? Out of the way, there's a good girl!"

I hastily skipped round the other side of the table. Dad hates to be crowded when he's in the kitchen. Mum says he's a bit of a prima donna.

"Do you think I could go to acting classes?" I said.

Dad said, "What sort of acting classes? Hand me the salt, would you?"

"*Acting* classes," I said. "*Drama*. At a *drama* school."

"Pepper!"

"It would give me poise," I said.

"Poise, eh? Taste this!" Dad thrust a spoon in my face. "How is it? Not too hot?"

44

"It's scrummy," I said. "The thing is, if I went to acting classes—"

"Bit more salt, I reckon."

"It would give me confidence, Dad!"

"Didn't know you lacked it," said Dad.

"I do," I said. "That's why I want to go. So could I, Dad? *Please*?"

"It's not up to me," said Dad. "Ask your mum."

I should have known! It's what he always says. Dad and me are really great mates, and he is wonderful for having cuddles with, but whenever it's anything serious he always, *always* says ask your mum. It's like Mum is the career woman, she is the big breadwinner, so she has to make all the decisions.

Well, of course, Mum didn't get in till late, and as usual she was worn to a frazzle and just wanted to go and soak in the bath.

"Darling, I'm exhausted!" she said. "It's been the most ghastly day. Let's talk at the weekend. We'll sit down and have a long chat, I promise."

"But, Mum," I said, "I need to talk *now*." Saffy would be cross if I didn't have an answer for her. She wanted us to be enrolled by the weekend. "All it is," I said, "I just want to know if I could go to drama classes."

It is easy to see how Mum has got ahead in business. In spite of being exhausted, she immediately wanted all the details, such as where, and who with, and how much.

Fortunately Saffy can be quite efficient when she puts her mind to it. She had told me where to find the advert in the Yellow Pages, plus she had written down all the things that Mum would want to know.

"It's right near where Saffy lives," I said. "I could go back with her after school on Fridays, and I thought perhaps you could come and pick me up afterwards. Maybe. I mean, if you weren't too busy. If you didn't have to work late. And then on Saturdays—"

"We could manage Saturdays between us," said Mum. "If you've really set your heart on it."

One of the *best* things about my mum is, when you do get to talk to her she doesn't keep you on tenterhooks while she hums and hahs and thinks things over. She makes up her mind right there and then. It's something I really like about her. Especially when she makes up her mind the way I want her to! Though considering Pip has his own computer and about nine million computer games, and Petal has her own TV and an iPod and a DS, and I don't have any of these things (mainly because I don't particularly want them) Mum probably thought that a few drama classes weren't so very much to ask. She is quite fair, on the whole, except for spoiling Pip rotten on account of him being the youngest. And of course a boy. I really do think boys get treated better than girls! Petal doesn't necessarily agree. She says that if Mum spoils Pip, then Dad spoils me. But he only spoils me with food. He'd spoil Petal with food if she'd let him, but she won't, so she only has herself to blame.

Anyway, Mum said that on Friday she would leave work early and come with me so that I could get myself enrolled. When she said that, I just nearly burst at the seams! I thought that for Mum to actually come with me was worth far more than if she'd bought me a dozen computers or TV sets. Mum works so hard and such long hours, she almost never gets to do anything with us. I couldn't resist a bit of boasting, on the phone to Saffy.

"Mum is going to come with me," I said.

"Yes, well, she'd have to," said Saffy. "Mine's coming, too. You have to have your parents' permission."

I couldn't really expect Saffy to understand how momentous it was, Mum leaving work early just for me. Saffy's mum only works part-time, and then all she does is answer someone's telephone. She's not high-powered like my mum! She is very nice, though. The sort of mum you read about in books. The sort that cooks and sews and all that stuff. Kind of... old-fashioned. Though I don't think Saffy sees it that way. She thinks it's quite normal to have a mum who's there in the morning when she leaves for school and there again in the afternoon when she gets back. She once told me that she found it a bit peculiar, me having a dad who stayed home to look after us.

"I wouldn't like that," she said.

When I asked her why not she couldn't really explain except to say that it wasn't natural. I said, "What do you mean, not natural?" Sounding, probably, a bit defensive. I mean, this was my mum and dad we were talking about! So then she wittered on about cavemen. How it was the cave*men* who went out and clubbed animals to death and dragged their carcasses back, while the cave*women* stayed in their caves doing the dusting and sweeping and making up beds.

She has some very odd ideas! That was back in the Stone Age. Does she think we haven't progressed?

As well as having odd ideas, I have to admit that Saffy does also have some good ones. Such as her brilliant plan for us to meet boys! As we got nearer to Friday, I found that I was growing quite excited. Partly it was the prospect of the gorgeous guys, but partly it was this feeling that I might be discovered. As a star, I mean! In spite of not being as show-offy as some people I could name, I have always had this secret belief that I could act far better than, for instance, an up-front in-your-face kind of person such as Dani Morris, who you can just bet your life will always be chosen for lead parts. I have simmered for *years* about Saffy being an angel and me not being anything. Even if I did have chicken pox and picked my spots. It wasn't as bad as all that! And anyway, what about make-up?

In case anyone is thinking ho, ho, you can't have plump angels, I would just beg to differ. I have seen plump angels! You only have to look at old paintings. There are loads of them. Plump angels, I mean. I would say that in those days you had more plump angels than you had thin ones. *But when did you ever see an angel with red hair?* I think that is a bit more to the point!

Not that I have anything against red hair, and certainly nothing against Saffy. It was just all this simmering that I'd been doing. Now at last I was coming to the boil! I saw myself on stage, acting a scene with one of the gorgeous guys. Holding hands... *kissing*. All the other gorge guys, who up until that point would not have looked twice at me, would suddenly be fancying me like crazy, thinking this girl is magnetic, this girl is just so-o-o sexy! And all the rest of them, all those cool kids that would have sneered when they first saw me – *oh, she is no competition! She is a nobody* – they would be, like, gobsmacked, wondering how come they could have got it so wrong. Even Saffy would be sitting there with her eyes on stalks. That's my friend Jenny? Jenny that I've known since Infants? That wasn't even cast as an angel?

Way to go!

The drama classes were held every Friday after school and every Saturday afternoon. Four hours a week! It sounds like a lot, but when you are doing something you enjoy it is truly amazing how quickly time passes. As opposed to how s-l-o-w-l-y it passes when it is something you positively loathe, such as maths, for example. Well, in my case when it is maths. I dare say there are some people, with the right sort of brains, that derive great pleasure from the subject.

Possibly not everyone would think it such fun to get up in front of other people and act out your deepest emotions, or do things which make you look foolish, but it is far more fun, to my way of thinking, than right-angled triangles or stupid problems about men filling baths with water. I was so pleased that Saffy had made us enrol! Why hadn't I thought of it? Saffy only wanted to meet boys; the acting bit was just an excuse. She didn't really care whether she was any good or not. I was the one with serious ambitions!

To be honest, I thought at first that I was going to be disappointed. It wasn't a bit how I'd expected it to be! I'd pictured a real school with a proper theatre and a dance studio, but all it was, was this shabby old house at the end of Saffy's road. The paintwork was all peeling, and the window sills were crumbling. Outside there was a sign that said **AMBROSE ACADEMY** in faded blue letters. The lady who ran it, Mrs Ambrose, was pretty faded, too. She had long white hair done in plaits on top of her head and looked even older than my grans.

I stared in dismay as me and Mum walked through the door that first Friday. I didn't mean to be rude, but how could this decrepit person be a drama teacher? I remember that I looked at Saffy and pulled a face, but Saffy just mouthed the one word: boys! It was all she cared about.

Mum obviously wasn't too impressed because when she came to fetch me, later that evening, she said, "Pumpkin, I'm sure there must be better places than this! Why don't we have a look round?"

I shrieked, "Mum, no!"

After only two hours, I was hooked. In spite of being so ancient, and having white hair, Mrs Ambrose was a true inspiration. She had this really *deep* voice, very commanding, and when she moved about the room it was like she was a ship on the sea, ploughing through the waves. She was strict, too! She didn't make you take auditions because she said that "drama is for everyone," but she did expect you to work. She said, "Some of you may go on to become professionals. Some of you are just here for fun. But even fun has to be taken seriously! Work hard and play hard and we can all enjoy ourselves." I think it came as a bit of a shock to Saffy, who'd probably imagined she was just going to slouch around ogling boys.

For the first half hour we did warm-ups. Physical ones, and ones for the voice.

Ay ee oo ah oo ee ay

MmmmmmmAhmmmmmmmEemmmmmmmEeeeeee

Sproo sprow spraw sprah spray spree

Saffy said afterwards that she found it a bit boring. I didn't! Mrs Ambrose said that I had a good strong voice and good breath control, and I could feel myself glowing. It is nice to be good at things! Saffy, on the other hand, was told that her voice was too tight and too squeaky and that she needed to loosen up, and she was given some special voice exercises to help her. I could see that Saffy wasn't too pleased, but as I pointed out to her, when she was moaning on about it, "There is no such thing as a free lunch."

"Meaning what?" said Saffy.

"Meaning," I said, "that if you want to meet boys you've got to work at it. You," I reminded her, "were the one that said so!"

"Huh!" said Saffy. And then, in pleading tones, she said, "I haven't really got a squeaky voice, have I?"

What could I say? Mrs Ambrose spoke the truth!

"This is so humiliating," wailed Saffy.

To comfort her, I said that it wasn't nearly so humiliating as turning right when you should have turned left, which was what happened to me while we were doing our warm-ups. I crashed slap, bang into this girl next to me.

She gave me such a glare! I have never been the athletic type, which was what made it so pathetic when I tried to join in with the sporty set. Mrs Ambrose said that I must work on my co-ordination, and the girl I crashed into muttered, "Yeah, and work on something else, as well!" eyeing me sourly as she did so. I wasn't sure what she meant by this cryptic  remark, so I decided to ignore it. I'd already said that I was sorry. What more did she want?

Everyone except me and Saffy was wearing black tights and black sweats, with *Ambrose Academy* printed on them. It was a sort of unofficial uniform, and I was already looking forward to wearing it on Saturday. Black is so flattering to the fuller figure. Saffy doesn't have a fuller figure, in fact she doesn't really have a figure at all, but she was looking forward to it because she thinks it is a mature sort of colour. Saffy is really anxious to be mature! (In case she happens to bump into Brad while he is between wives, I guess.)

After we'd finished voice exercises we all settled down to work on this soap that we were creating. The title, which was *Sob Story*, had already been decided on before me and Saffy enrolled. It was about three girls who were trying to make it as an all-girl band. One of the boys was their manager, and another was a record producer, and one was a DJ. All the rest were friends and neighbours. Saffy and me had to invent characters for ourselves. Saffy decided that she would be "someone from America".

"Doing what?" said the girl I'd crashed into.

"Just visiting," said Saffy.

"Why?" said the girl.

"Why not?" said Saffy.

Angrily, the girl said, "It doesn't play any part in the storyline!"

"How do you know?" said Saffy.

Well, of course, she didn't. She subsided, muttering. I felt quite proud of Saffy! She is not a person who will let herself be pushed around.

"What about you?" said the girl, looking at me like I was a drip on the end of someone's nose.

I said that I was going to be an old person. Mrs Ambrose cried, "Good! That's good! Someone brave enough to do a bit of real acting."

The girl gave me this *look*. I could tell already that she didn't like me. As a rule I am such a creepy crawly that it really upsets me if I feel I am not liked. I want to be liked by everyone! But you can't be; not if you have any sort of personality, which I think I *do* have. When I can get it sorted out! When I stop trying to be all these other things. But anyway, for once in my life it didn't really bother me. I was having too good a time being this old person! I made up a name for myself, Mrs Fuzzle, and I went round complaining about pop music being just a horrible noise, and not like it was when when I was young.

I based it on one of my grans! Dad's mum, who is nearly seventy and says that nothing is the same as it used to be. (Mum's mum is younger and more with it.) Dad's mum doesn't grouch; she isn't one of those nasty cross old people. But my one was! Mrs Fuzzle. She spoke all the time in this whiny kind of voice.

"You kids today... no manners! No consideration for the old folk. It wasn't like this when I was young. When I was young we had respect. We had proper music, too! Not all this head-banging muck."

I found myself wandering into every scene, doing my complaining. I even managed to get into the recording studio! It wasn't exactly what I'd had in mind. I wasn't acting scenes of mad passion with a gorgeous guy, and people going ooh and aah and being gobsmacked.

But everyone laughed, and the boy playing the record producer couldn't speak for corpsing!

"You were showing off," said Saffy, when we met up next day.

I didn't mean to show off. I am not a showing-off kind of person! I'd never realised before that I could make people laugh. Even Saffy agreed that it had been funny.

"But not very glam," she said.

She pointed out that next term, when we were going to record *Sob Story* on video, I would have to dress up as an old woman and paint wrinkles on my face. I hadn't thought of that!

"It's all right," said Saffy. "It just means you're a *character* actress."

But I didn't want to be a character actress! I wanted to be beautiful and attract boys! For a while I was crestfallen, thinking that I had made a big mistake. Everyone else was going to be cool and funky, and I was going to be an aged old hag with wrinkles! And then I had this bright idea.

"I know!" I said. "I'll do a transformation scene!"

Saffy blinked and said, "What?"

"At the end... like in pantomime! I'll have this mask and I'll tear it off, and I'll jump out of my coat and I'll be the good fairy with a magic wand that makes everyone's wishes come true!"

Saffy looked at me with what I felt was new respect.

"That," she said, "is just brilliant!"

I thought it was, too. I thought, I've got what it takes! It is very important to have what it takes. You can't get anywhere if you haven't got it. But I had! I was going places. I had discovered my vocation!

"You've got to admit," said Saffy, "that it was a good idea of mine, wasn't it?"

"It was my idea!" I said.

"No, you twonk!" She gave me a companionable biff on the arm. "Going to drama school."

"Oh! That," I said. "Yes." I beamed at her. "It was one of the best ideas you've ever had!"

four

IT WAS JUST *so good* to have
found something I could do, other
than drawing pictures of the rabbit's
reproductive system (which now
seemed rather gross). I could act! I could make people
laugh! I had a good strong voice! I had good breath
control! It made me feel all bubbly and enthusiastic, so
much so that I actually started doing voice exercises
every evening in my bedroom.

Ay ee oo ah oo ee ay
Mummy mummy mummy mummy
MmmmmAH! MmmmmmAY! MmmmmmEE!

Then there were the little stories, about Witty Kitty McQuitty, and Carlotta's Past, and Cook with her pudding basins. They were all for different vowel sounds, and I practised them like crazy.

Witty Kitty McQuitty was a natty secretary to Sir Willy Gatty mmmmmAH! MmmmmmAY! MmmmmmEE!

One day I opened my bedroom door to find Pip crouching there with his ear to the keyhole. Well, it obviously *had* been to the keyhole. You could tell.

"What do you want?" I said.

Pip said, "Who were you talking to?"

I said, "What business is it of yours? Can't a person have a private conversation in this house?"

Pip said it hadn't sounded like a conversation. "Sounded more like a cow farting."

Greatly annoyed, I said, "When did you ever hear a cow fart?"

"Just now," said Pip. "In your bedroom!"

"You shouldn't have been listening!" I screeched.

"Couldn't help it," said Pip, "the racket you were making."

He then galloped off downstairs going "Moo! Moo! Fart!" and making silly waggling motions with his fingers.

"Moron!" I shouted; but he just stuck out his tongue and fled along the hall.

I thought to myself that considering he was supposed

to be some kind of genius, his behaviour could be quite extraordinarily childish. But then, of course, he *was* only ten years old. I think sometimes we tended to forget that. It is probably quite normal, at ten years old, to be stupid and annoying. I just didn't want him being stupid and annoying about my voice exercises!

I was really determined to take this thing seriously. The acting, I mean. At the back of my mind I was already thinking that maybe, when I left school, I could go to a proper drama academy. One of the big ones, up in London! They'd just had the film awards on television and I'd seen myself, in a few years' time, stepping on stage to collect my Oscar for Best Actress.

The self that I saw was tall and willowy, verree sexy, wearing this slinky designer dress. Black with silver sequins, and a slit down the side. The dress would not only show a lot of leg, but a lot of everything else, as well, because by then I would have a figure worth flaunting. ie, *thin*. This was my daydream! But it was precious, and it was fragile, and I didn't need my little genius brother shattering it for me.

I hugged my daydream all to myself. I didn't even tell Saffy! I knew she wouldn't laugh, as we are never unkind to each other; but I had this feeling that beneath the polite exterior she would probably be going, "Yeah yeah yeah!" just as I do when she starts on about Brad. I do it to humour her. But that is different. Saffy must know, deep down inside herself, that her feelings for Brad are just fantasy. This was my whole future!

I remembered how Saffy herself had said this, when she was instructing me what to say to Mum. "Tell her your entire future is at stake." A premonition! I thought that when I was famous I would have a lot to thank Saffy for, and I immediately added an extra bit to my Best Actress scene.

In the new, extended version I didn't just waft on to stage in my slinky black dress to collect my award, I actually gave an acceptance speech in which I graciously referred to "My best friend, Saffy." Saffy would be there, in the audience. She would blush and clasp her hands to her cheeks as the camera zoomed in on her. She would be looking very chic but not too beautiful. Afterwards, I would invite her to join my party for a celebratory dinner in a posh restaurant, one where all the stars went. Maybe Brad would be there! He would walk past our table and catch sight of me and do this huge double-take and go, "Jen! Baby! Congratulations!" Then he would give me a big kiss on my cheek. And I would be very cool and laid back and say, "Brad, I'd like you to meet my friend Saffy. Saffy, I'm sure you recognise Brad Pitt?" And he would take her hand and say, "Hi there, Saffy!" and she would just nearly die.

Oh, it was such a beautiful dream! Far more exciting than any of my others. I simply couldn't *imagine* what had ever made me think I would like to be a car mechanic! It is without doubt an extremely useful occupation but I don't think anyone could call it glamorous and I have never heard of any Best Car Mechanic Awards, though of course there may be, there may even be Oscars, only it is not done on television and you would probably not get many of the mechanics wearing slinky black dresses and showing their legs. But it is a nice thought!

Not many of the boys at the Academy looked like they would ever become car mechanics. I don't think I am being unfair to car mechanics when I say that on the whole you don't expect them to be especially sensitive and creative sort of people. Then again, of course, I could be wrong. Just because a person likes to lie upside down beneath cars and stick his head into their engines, and get covered all over in oily black gunge, doesn't necessarily mean they are not sensitive. Or creative. I am sure you can be very creative inside a car engine. It is just a different sort of creative. That is all.

One thing Saffy was right about, we didn't have any boys like Nathan Corrie. Thank goodness! They weren't all gorgeous, but at least they all came from this planet. One or two of them were actually quite geeky, not to mention goofy, and even what I would call plain. But they weren't boring! What I mean is, they had *personality*. Plus they could talk about stuff other than football or computers. You could have real proper conversations with them, like discussing what you had just done in class or a new scene you'd worked out for *Sob Story*. I really enjoyed doing that! I'd never thought of boys as being people you had conversations with.

Some of them were quite funny. The boys, I mean. There was this one boy, Robert Phillips, who couldn't pronounce his Rs and had to keep reciting *Round the ragged rocks the ragged rascal ran.* It always came out as "Wound the wagged wocks," which drove Mrs Ambrose to despair. On the other hand, she said there was quite a demand, these days, for "upper class English twits" in Hollywood movies, so maybe he could turn his speech impediment to good use.

I personally found it quite difficult to picture Robert as a movie star, but Saffy, in her wise way, said that stranger things had happened. I was just glad that I didn't have any kind of speech impediment. Mrs Ambrose said the only sound I had to work on was the "oo" sound and she told me to practise "the moon in June" and *mmmmmOO*. I made sure only to do it when Pip was downstairs and safely out of earshot!

Another boy who was a bit geeky was Ben Azariah. He had a head like a turnip! His hair grew *upwards*, to a point. He did this thing of twizzling it with his finger which made us all laugh! In spite of being geeky, he was totally brilliant as a mimic. He could do Ant and Dec really well. He could also do this famous footballer that I won't name in case it might count as libel, plus loads others, who I also won't name, because I mean you just never know. Celebs can be really touchy. Mum says they will sue you at the drop of a hat. I wouldn't want that!

Another person Ben could do was Mrs Ambrose. He had us all in stitches being her.

"Robert, my *deah* boy! You really must learn to pronounce your Rs!"

I certainly couldn't imagine Ben being a big

Hollywood star, but I could easily see him having his own TV show. Saffy agreed. She added that when people were a bit odd-looking, they often turned to humour. She said, "It's a defence mechanism."

I found this rather worrying and immediately rushed home to examine myself in the mirror and see if I was funny-looking, and if that was why I had chosen to play an old person in *Sob Story*, so that I could make people laugh and they would stop noticing how weird I was.

But I thought on the whole I was OK. I didn't have a head like a turnip, my hair didn't grow to a point. I even thought, secretly – I mean, trying to pretend to myself that I wasn't thinking it, as it seemed rather vain – that I had nice eyes. They are bright blue, like Petal's. Dani Morris once asked me if I wore coloured contact lenses, because she said you couldn't have eyes that were as blue as that, it wasn't natural. Well, it is, and I do! So sucks to Dani Morris.

All the same, I was glad that I'd hit on the transformation scene. Under my baggy old lady coat I intended to wear something really sensational. I hadn't yet decided what, since it was still a long way off, but even when I had I was going to keep it a secret so that everyone would be taken by surprise and go "Ooooh!"

There were two people I specially wanted to go "Ooooh". Both of them were boys. Surprise, surprise! There was Gareth Hartley, who was the one that had corpsed when I wandered into the recording studio doing my complaining, and there was Mark Nelson, who played the DJ. Both were truly cool! Everything that Saffy had promised. Creative and sensitive and *seriously gorgeous*.

Mark was like the big star. He had once been in a movie and had had real lines to say! Everyone fancied him like crazy. Even Saffy said that he was "lip-smacking" (what kind of disgusting expression is that?). She said that she would actually be prepared to accept him as a substitute while she was waiting for Brad to get divorced. But "Some hopes!" she added.

I told her that she could always dream, though as she was already dreaming about Brad I thought perhaps I could be the one to dream about Mark. I knew it was a dream that couldn't ever really come true. Gorgeous guys, especially when they are nearly seventeen, don't very often fall for plump twelve year olds, even if the plump twelve year olds do have bright blue eyes. Maybe when I'd taken the world by storm doing my transformation scene... Well, anyway. We would see!

In the mean time, there was always Gareth. He wasn't quite as gorgeous as Mark, but on the other hand he was only fourteen, so I thought perhaps I might stand a bit more of a chance. Saffy said he wasn't really mature enough for her, but that he would do "if all else failed." She had some nerve!

One thing she'd been wrong about, and that was the girls. She'd promised me they wouldn't all be gorgeous, and it was true they weren't *all*, but lots of them were! Even the ones that weren't were just so-o-o cool. And guess what? They were all thin! Thin as pins. All except for Connie Foster, who was little and bouncy and could walk on her hands and do the splits and pick up her leg and pull it straight up into the air, as far as her head. I would love to be able to do that! If I could do that I would be doing it all the time, just to show off. The only reason I don't show off is that I have nothing to show off about. What I mean is, it is not a *virtue*.

Connie was the same age as me and Saffy and really nice. I'm not just saying that because she was the only person who wasn't thin, but because she was sweet and giggly, and *she* didn't show off, either. Not like some of them! Angie Moon, for example. She was the most horrible show-off. She had this habit of twinkling, by which I mean she would suddenly open her eyes very wide and stretch her lips into this great mindless grimace with her top teeth showing. I think it was supposed to be a smile. She did it whenever a boy happened to look at her, and especially Mark or Gareth. Me and Saffy thought it was pathetic. Saffy started calling her Little Miss Twinkle, which soon got shortened to just Twinkle, or Twink. She never understood why we called her that! She probably thought it was a compliment, as she had a very high opinion of herself.

Another girl who thought she was the cat's whiskers was Zoë Davidson. She was the one I crashed into when I got my left muddled up with my right and turned the wrong way. She had an even higher opinion of herself than Twinkle. This wasn't because she was specially gorgeous, it was because she'd been on television and had recently done a commercial for something-or-other,

I have forgotten what as thankfully I never saw it. Saffy did. She said it was nauseating.

"Vomit-making! Pukey! *Yuck*!"

Even though Zoë wasn't one of the gorgeous ones, I suppose she was sort of cheeky-looking. She had what Mrs Ambrose called "a televisual face". The sort of face that can be filmed from almost any angle.

"Either the camera likes you or it doesn't."

That was what *she* said. Zoë. Talk about loving yourself! She really reckoned she was some kind of star. Not that she was the only one who'd been on the telly or appeared in commercials. Several of the kids had. Mark had even been in the West End! But he didn't boast about it. Zoë just really fancied herself. Everyone said she was going to go places; even Saffy. Saffy said, "She's the sort that does."

She said that you had to be a bit big-headed and pushy and think a lot of yourself, because if you didn't think a lot of yourself then who else would?

I wondered if this was true. If so, I found it rather depressing. More than anything else in the world I wanted to have loads of confidence; but I didn't want to be big-headed and pushy! Did this mean I wouldn't ever get anywhere? I asked Saffy and she said it depended where I wanted to get. She said, "I expect you could probably get somewhere if you just wanted to do something ordinary, like working in a shop. But not if you wanted to be a big movie star."

My face must have fallen, because she then added comfortingly that that was all right because I didn't want to be a big movie star, did I?

"It's not what we came for," she said. "You know what we came for!" And she pulled a face and jerked her head and rolled her eyes in the direction of a group of boys on the opposite side of the street. (We were on our way to Friday classes at the time.) "*That's* what we came for... right?"

I said, "Right. But I wouldn't actually mind being a movie star!"

It just, like, blurted out before I could stop it. I thought for a dreadful moment that Saffy was going to laugh, but she is my friend and we always take each other seriously. After all, I had taken her seriously when she once confided in me that she thought she would like to be a missionary and go round converting people. Which was really quite funny considering she was the one who was sent out of an RE class for having an unseemly fit of the giggles at what Miss Cooper called "a totally inappropriate moment". (She has now decided that it is wrong to try and convert people as she feels they are probably quite happy left as they are. And, in any case, she is an atheist.)

"Do you think I'm being stupid?" I said.

Saffy said that it was never stupid to be ambitious and want to get on in life.

"Yes, but do you think I stand any chance?" I said.

Bracingly Saffy said that everybody stood a chance.

70

"It depends how determined you are."

"I'm very determined," I said. I was. I really was! I could see a whole glorious future unfolding before me.

"Well, this is what's important," said Saffy. "Knowing what you want and going for it."

"Even though I don't have much confidence?" I said.

Saffy told me that I had got to get confidence. She said there was no reason why I shouldn't have it.

"You know you can speak OK, Mrs A's always holding you up as an example. And you do have confidence when you get up and act."

I said, "It's different when you're acting. You're being someone else."

"But what about when you have to go for auditions?" said Saffy.

We'd been learning about auditions just recently from Mrs Ambrose. How to prepare ourselves, and what to wear, and stuff like that.

"You've got to have confidence being *you*," said Saffy. "I can't think why you don't! I would if I were you."

"It's all right for you," I said. "You're thin!"

"Yes," said Saffy, "but you're pretty."

I felt my face turn bright pink. It was the nicest thing she'd ever said to me! I felt quite touched and immediately began trying to think of something I could say to her in return.

"I'd rather be skinny like you," I said.

"Then you wouldn't have boobs," said Saffy. "You have to have boobs to be a movie star." She sighed. "I don't suppose I'll ever have any."

It's true that her mum hasn't; not to speak of. But Petal has, and she is skinny! I said this to Saffy, but she said that Petal was slim, not skinny. She said the two were not the same.

"Skinny is thin and scrawny; slim is when you've got some shape."

"Like Twinkle," I said. I think you have to be honest about these things. I didn't like her very much, but she did have a figure to die for.

"Yes," said Saffy, "but that's *all* she's got. She can't act to save her life!"

"She's been in a commercial," I said.

"Well, you know why," said Saffy. "It's 'cos she's pushy! Her and Zoë. They're both the same. It doesn't mean they can *act*."

Now that she mentioned it, I knew that she was right. About them being pushy, I mean. They were always elbowing and shoving, to get themselves up front.

Saffy said, "You gotta face it, babe! It's the way it's done."

I looked at her, doubtfully. I'm not a very shoving sort of person. I wanted to be discovered – but not by pushing myself forward! I wanted someone to come along and simply stare right through the likes of Zoë and Twink.

"Who is that girl at the back?" they would say. "The one with those startling blue eyes?"

Everyone would turn and stare. Mrs Ambrose would say, "That's Jenny... one of our little stars."

And I would be told to come out to the front and I would be signed up right there and then for this big part on telly, and Zoë and Twink would gnash their teeth and feel utterly humiliated. Ho ho!

"Babe, you gotta get real," said Saffy, in this accent she fondly believes is American. "It's no use hiding your light under a flowerpot, or whatever it is. You gotta, like, go up to people and say, *I'm Jenny Penny! Take notice of me!*"

"Just like that?" I said, alarmed.

"Well, not in so many words," said Saffy. "But you can't let people like that stupid Twinkle elbow you out the way! Just remember, you're as good as she is any day."

I thought to myself that Saffy can sometimes be so wise, and so clever. I *was* as good as Twinkle! Twinkle couldn't act to save her life. The only way she'd got to be a member of the all-girl band in *Sob Story* was by pushing and shoving. She couldn't sing, she couldn't dance, she couldn't even speak properly. She had this silly little girly voice, all high-pitched and tinny.

Zoë couldn't really sing, either, but she was one of those people, when she was on stage you found yourself having to look at her even if you didn't specially want to. I certainly didn't want to! Not after the way she'd been so horrid when I'd accidentally bumped into her. She'd gone on being horrid, for days afterwards. She kept saying things like, "Ever had a ten-ton trailer crash into you?" and "Keep away from me, Elephant!" So you can see that I had absolutely *no* reason to watch her, yet in spite of that I couldn't seem to help it. Which meant, I suppose, that she had got "what it takes".

But so had Mark and Gareth, and they didn't push and shove! Gareth was quite up-front, but he never *bulldozed*. And Mark was cool as could be! He had this very quiet sort of confidence, which I really envied. I thought that I would try to have a quiet confidence, too. I thought it might be easier than pushing and shoving. So when we all lined up that evening for our workout, I very firmly – but *quietly* – positioned myself at the front and waited to see what would happen.

Like normally, not being a show-offy kind of person, as I think I have said before, I would hide away at the back along with Saffy and Ben and a tall gangly girl called Portia, who was really sweet and tried *so* hard but just could never get anything right. Zoë always referred to her as Stilts, because of her legs being so long. I was Elephant, Portia was Stilts, and Saffy was Beetroot Bonce (on account of her red hair). Me and Saffy had racked our brains trying to think of a rude nickname for Zoë but hadn't yet come up with anything.

So, anyway, there I was, minding my own business, quietly doing stretchy exercises while waiting for class to begin, and guess what happens? Zoë comes waltzing up and rudely plants herself *directly in front of me*. Next thing I know, Little Miss Twinkle has joined her. And before I can say anything, such as "Excuse *me*!" or "Do you mind?" the door has opened and the boys have come in and Gareth and a couple of others have tacked themselves next to Zoë and Twinkle, so that now *they're* the front row and I'm pushed into the background. I mean, it wasn't Gareth's fault. He didn't know that Zoë had deliberately usurped me. When Mrs Ambrose arrived she told everyone to "Move back! You're too far out!" Zoë immediately sprang backwards, managing to tread on my toe as she did so. She said, "Oops! Sorry, Elephant, didn't know you were there." *That girl!* Is it any wonder she got on our nerves?

Saffy, of course, had seen what was happening. Saffy is very sharp. She doesn't miss much! She rang me later, when Mum had come to collect me and I was back home.

"You see what I mean?" she said. "You see what I mean about pushing and shoving? You gotta get your act together, babe!"

I said that I would try, but that it was very difficult when we were, like, the new girls on the block and Zoë and Twinkle had been there practically for ever.

"You think that would stop *them*?" said Saffy.

I had to admit that it probably wouldn't, and I humbly promised Saffy that in future I would stand up for myself. I knew she only had my best interests at heart. All the same, she is the most terrible bully!

five

ONE FRIDAY, MRS Ambrose told us that an old pupil of the school, Deirdre Dobson, was going to come in the next day and talk to us about acting and maybe even watch a class. I was so excited! A lot of people hadn't heard of Deirdre Dobson, but I had because I had *met* her. It was a long time ago, when I was quite young, but I could still remember this lovely lady with the jet black hair and silver rings. She came into my mum's office when for some reason I was there, and she actually talked to Mum about this house she was thinking of buying. Mum told me afterwards, "That was Deirdre Dobson!" Then when she got home she told Dad about it.

"Guess who came into the office today? Deirdre Dobson!"

Then she rang up both my grans and one of my aunties and told them about it, too, so I knew that Deirdre Dobson had to be somebody famous. Mum was always talking about "the time I sold a house to Deirdre Dobson", though it was a year or two before I realised that this famous person was an actress on television. She was in a soap called *Screamers*, which I was too young ever to have watched. It had finished about four years ago, which was why most of the kids had never heard of her. They were well impressed when I said that I had actually met her! Zoë immediately said that *she* had met Tom Cruise, but we had all heard about Zoë meeting Tom Cruise about a million times, and anyway she hadn't met him, she'd merely seen him at a distance.

"What's she like?" said Twinkle.

I said that I remembered her as being very slim and beautiful with dark black hair. Zoë sniffed and said, "She's probably an old bag by now. *I've* never heard of her."

"Just shows the depths of *your* ignorance," said Saffy; not that Saffy had ever heard of her, either.

I told Mum about it when she came to pick me up after class. Mum said, "Oh! Tell her that your mum once sold her a house. Ask her if she's still living there... Clonmore Gardens. Mind, it was a few years ago. She probably won't remember."

"I met her," I said, "didn't I?"

"Yes, you did," said Mum. "You were sitting on my desk, playing with the paper clips... very unprofessional! Miss Dobson said what lovely blue eyes you had."

"*Did* she?" I squirmed with a sort of pleasurable embarrassment. "Was she nice?"

"She was all right," said Mum. "I always find actors a bit gushy."

But she had said how lovely my eyes were! I wondered if she would remember, and whether I would be brave enough to remind her. I don't mean about my eyes, but about my sitting on Mum's desk playing with the paper clips, and Mum selling her a house. Saturday morning I rang Saffy to ask her advice.

"Do you think I ought to remind her, or would that be too pushy?"

Saffy screamed, "J*ennee*! It isn't possible to be too pushy... not if you want to get somewhere. How many times do I have to tell you?"

She said that if I didn't go and introduce myself to Miss Dobson she would disown me.

"All right," I said. "I'll do it!"

"You'd better," said Saffy. "'Cos I will disown you... I mean it!"

Miss Dobson was there, talking to Mrs Ambrose, when we arrived for class. I very shyly smiled at her as I came in, but she gave no sign of recognising me. But then of course she must have met thousands of people since seeing me on Mum's desk, and probably some of them would have had blue eyes like mine. And in any case I had done quite a lot of growing up since then.

Miss Dobson had done some growing up, too. She wasn't anywhere near as slender as I remembered, but her hair was still jet black, in fact it was even blacker than ever, and she still wore her lovely silver rings on every finger and was still quite glamorous. I was so glad she wasn't an old bag! If she had been, Zoë would have crowed like crazy.

Mrs Ambrose told us how Miss Dobson had been one of her very first pupils, way back when.

"Many years ago, when I was young. Because even I was young once," said Mrs Ambrose. We all laughed, politely, but Miss Dobson just gave this rather small tight smile. I thought perhaps she wasn't too happy at Mrs Ambrose saying how she had been a pupil "many years ago". Probably she would rather we thought it was just a short while back.

"Now, what I propose," said Mrs Ambrose, "I propose we show Miss Dobson how we do our warm-up exercises, and after that she's very kindly agreed to give us a talk, all about her experiences as an actor. So!" She clapped her hands. "Shall we get started?"

We headed off across the studio. I deliberately moved at a tortoise-like pace, thinking to myself that if I got there *last*, I would in fact be at the front. Only it didn't work out that way. The minute I stopped, Zoë and Twinkle, *in unison*, rudely elbowed their way past me and took up their usual prominent positions where they could be sure of being seen. Everyone else then shuffled forward to join them, with the result that I ended up – also as usual – at the back. Saffy poked me in the ribs and hissed, "*Push!*" But I couldn't. It was too late, it would have looked too obvious. I didn't want to be obvious.

It was probably just as well since I was so shaky with nerves I would most likely have done something stupid like turning the wrong way and bumping into Zoë all over again. At least at the back if I turned the wrong way it wouldn't be so noticeable. Actually, I didn't, but the point is I *could* have done. Being me. I thought that when it came to voice exercises I would be all right. Then I would be noticed, even at the back! But we didn't ever get to voice exercises because Mrs Ambrose said that now Miss Dobson was going to talk to us, and we all had to sit on the floor and listen.

I was disappointed at not being able to show how well I could do *hoo hoh haw* and *sproo spray spree*, but I did find the talk interesting. She told us all about being a pupil with Mrs Ambrose and how she had gone on to a full-time drama school when she was seventeen. She told us about "early struggles" and "bad times" when she had had to do all kinds of different jobs, such as for example being a waitress and scrubbing floors, to earn a living. She told us how her big break had come when she was chosen to play a part in *Screamers*. She had been in it for ten years. *Ten years!* A sort of gasp went up. Ten years was almost as long as some of us had lived!

Finally, she told us that the acting profession was the finest profession in the world, but that you had to be tough if you wanted to survive. Mrs Ambrose said, "Hear, hear! I second that," and Saffy poked me in the ribs, *again*, and hissed, "See?"

To end up we had a question and answer session when lots of people wanted to know how to get into drama school full time and which drama school to try for, and Zoë told everybody how she'd already been in two commercials and a television show, and Saffy kept

poking and poking until I
thought I would scream. I
hissed, "*Stop it!*" and she
hissed, "*Say something!*"
and I hissed, "*Not
yet!*" I didn't want
to do it in front of
everyone. After all, it
was personal.

I waited till the session had finished and Mark had
said thank you on behalf of all of us and Miss Dobson
was putting her coat on. Then I scuttled across the room
– propelled by a particularly vicious jab from Saffy –
and breathlessly, before I could get cold feet, gabbled,
"Miss Dobson, my name's Jenny Penny and my mum
helped you buy your house in Clonmore Gardens!"

There was a pause, then she looked at me, sort of...
not in the least bit interested, and said, "Really? That
must have been a while ago."

"I was six," I said. "I was sitting on my mum's desk
and you said hallo to me."

"I'm afraid I have no memory of it," said Miss Dobson.
"I've lived in so many different places since then."

"Oh. Mum wanted to know if you were still there," I said.

"No," said Miss Dobson. "I'm not!"

I could see that she wanted to leave, but now that I'd
started I just didn't seem able to stop.

"I really enjoyed your talk," I said.

"Good," said Miss Dobson. "That's good."

"You told us so many interesting things!"

"Well, you know... one doesn't like to be boring."

"Oh, you weren't *boring*," I assured her. "It was just, like, incredibly fascinating! To hear all about when you were young, and – and being out of work and everything."

Miss Dobson gave another of her tight little smiles.

"Honestly," I said, "I found it truly inspiring!"

"I'm glad to hear that," said Miss Dobson. "Now, if you'll excuse me—"

She opened the door, and I raced round in front of her.

"I know it was a very long time ago and things have changed, like you said how you got a grant to go to drama school and these days you probably couldn't, but—" I beamed up at her. "It's what I want to do! More than anything... I want to be an actress!"

"You do?" said Miss Dobson.

I nodded rapturously. I had done it! I had talked to her! Saffy would be so pleased with me.

"You want to be an actress?" Miss Dobson was eyeing me up and down, as if weighing my chances. "Well, my dear, the best advice I can give you," she said, "is to shed some of that excess baggage you're carrying."

A terrible hush fell over the room. Everyone just, like, froze. Including me. Normally if I am embarrassed I will go all hot and red, but this time I did the exact opposite. I went very cold and could feel my cheeks turn white and fungussy. At the same time I broke out into a sweat. It was like someone had just punched me in the stomach. I couldn't believe that Miss Dobson would say such a thing!

Mrs Ambrose was the only person who hadn't heard. She'd gone into the small room next to the studio and now came beaming back, all unaware, carrying this huge bouquet of flowers.

"Jenny!" she said. "Give these to Miss Dobson with one of your very best curtseys!"

If I could have guessed, just ten minutes earlier, that I would be the one chosen out of all the class to present Miss Dobson with her bouquet, I would have been so excited. I would have been so proud! *Me*, of all people! But I knew that Mrs Ambrose had only picked me because I happened to be standing there, not because I was special. I wobbled down into a curtsey, on legs that had gone all weak and bendy, and thrust the bouquet upwards while keeping my eyes glued to the floor. I then overbalanced and sat down, with a thump, on my bottom.

Nobody laughed. Mrs Ambrose said, "Well! That wasn't the most gracious of presentations, but never mind. These things happen."

She then said that she was going to escort Miss Dobson to her car.

"When I get back we'll just run the first few scenes of *Sob Story*."

The minute the door closed, everyone came flocking round me. It was terrible. They were all so nice!

"She didn't have to say that," said Mark. "That was a rotten thing to say."

"It was really mean!" said Connie.

"Even if it's true," agreed Twinkle. "She still shouldn't have said it."

"What d'you mean?" Saffy rounded on her. "*Even if it's true?*"

"Well—" Twinkle fluffed and huffed and looked a bit embarrassed.

"Jenny isn't *fat*," said Saffy.

"No, she's not," said Portia. Portia is thin as a piece of string. I'm sure she did think I was fat, really; she was just trying to make me feel better.

Gareth said that the whole conversation was becoming fattist. He said there were loads of fat actresses.

"*And* actors," said Ben.

"Yes, but it's worse for women," said Twinkle.

Saffy said, "Why?"

"It just is."

"It is!" Zoë did a little skinny twirl. "It's far worse. It's so unfair!"

"You could always do voice-overs," said Robert.

"Or radio," said Twinkle. "It wouldn't matter what you looked like on radio."

"Of course, you know why she said it?" said Zoë.

I said, "W-why?" Thinking that Zoë, in her mean way, would say something horrid such as, "Because it's the truth, Elephant!" But she didn't. She said, "'Cos she was feeling ratty!" Zoë twirled, triumphantly. "'Cos she used to be somebody and now she isn't and nobody's heard of her!"

Everyone nodded and went "Yeah! Right!" They were all on my side, even the Terrible Two, and I suppose that did help a little bit, but it couldn't stop me feeling utterly downcast and dejected. I thought, this is what happens when I try to have confidence. I wished so much that I had never spoken to Miss Dobson!

I went back afterwards for tea with Saffy. I told her that I wished I'd never gone and introduced myself.

"You mustn't let it get to you," urged Saffy.

"But she said I was fat!"

"She didn't, actually," said Saffy.

"She said excess baggage! It means the same thing. It means I'm *fat*."

"Jen, you're not!" said Saffy.

"I'm not thin," I said.

"So what?" said Saffy. "Who says you have to be thin to be an actress?"

I challenged her. I said, "Tell me one that isn't! A *young* one."

She couldn't, of course. Because I just bet there aren't any! I defy anyone to make a Top Ten of Fat Actresses Under the Age of Thirty.

"Well, anyway," said Saffy, "she had some nerve! She's not exactly a skeleton."

"She's not under thirty," I said.

"No, more like fifty," said Saffy.

She was still thinner than I was.

Mum called round at seven o'clock to fetch me. She said, "We're all going up the road to have a pizza. How was Miss Dobson? Did you talk to her?"

I said, "Mm," hoping Mum wouldn't want to pursue the subject. But naturally she did.

"Is she still living in Clonmore Gardens? Did she remember meeting you? What was she like? What did you talk about?"

I heaved a sigh. I said, "She doesn't live there any more and she didn't really remember but we didn't have time to talk very much, and I'm not sure that I feel like a pizza."

"Oh? That's unlike you," said Mum. "Well, you don't have to have a pizza! You can have whatever you want. You can have pasta, you can—"

"Not sure I feel like anything," I said.

But by the time we'd collected Petal and Pip and walked up the road to Giorgio's, I'd changed my mind. I not only had a pizza, one of Dad's specials, I also had garlic bread with cheese on top and a *big* helping of tiramisu. Food can be a real comfort when you're feeling low.

Unfortunately, lovely though it is at the time, food isn't what you would call a *permanent* source of comfort. It doesn't really last very long. It's all right while you're actually eating it and thinking to yourself, "Yum yum!" and not caring about the rest of the world and what you might look like; but then after a bit it starts to go down, and you go down as well.

Sometimes you are in such despair that you have to go and eat even more food to bring yourself back up again, which was why I went and raided the fridge the minute we got back home. But *that* didn't help, because I just went straight up to my bedroom and burst into tears.

I forced myself to look in the mirror, the full-length one on the inside of my wardrobe door, and I just HATED what I saw. This great fat... *pumpkin.* All round and bloated. How could I ever think of being an actress?

How could I ever take my clothes off in front of a camera? How could I dance? Who was going to pay money to go and watch a great fat thing flolloping about? Ugh! I wouldn't!

As a rule when I am down I do my best to bounce back up, and usually I succeed. Maybe it is one of the advantages of being plump: you can bounce in a way that thin people can't. Well, that is my theory.

This time it took me the whole of Sunday before I managed to bounce. I ate eggs, mushrooms-and-tomatoes *and* cereal *and* toast-and-marmalade for breakfast, a big helping of lasagne and an even bigger helping of chocolate pudding for lunch, buttered crumpets and lemon meringue pie for tea and pistachio ice cream for supper, after which I felt a bit better. I decided that I would just *show* that Deirdre Dobson!

I told Saffy at break on Monday, and Saffy said it was good that I was thinking positively. She said Deirdre Dobson deserved to be shown.

"Stinky old bag!"

I said she wasn't an old bag *yet*, but I thought she probably would be in a few years' time.

"Yes, and by then," said Saffy, "you'll be a big star! You'll be on the way up, and she'll be on the way down!"

I immediately had a mental picture of a ladder, with me – slim as a pin, and dressed to kill – zooming up to the top, and Deirdre Dobson – all saggy and baggy and fat – on the great slide to the bottom. I was heading for the bright lights: *she* was going to the trash heap. We would pass each other and I would smile, ever so graciously, and wave.

"I shan't gloat," I said to Saffy, "because that would be demeaning."

"But you could remind her," said Saffy. "You know, just casually. You could say, *Who's the fat one now, then?*"

We giggled.

"She might even beg to be in one of your movies," said Saffy. "Would you let her?"

"I might," I said, "if she humbled herself."

"You could say, *Oh, yes, there is a part here for an old fat bag...* that's how it would appear in the cast list," said Saffy. "Old Fat Bag!"

We had a lot of fun, inventing parts that Deirdre Dobson could play in my movies. Old Fat Bag, Toothless Hag, Wizened Granny, Fat Woman in Bikini. I felt good. I felt strong. I would show her!

I ate a plate of chips and a doughnut at lunchtime to keep up the good feelings, and a packet of crisps during afternoon break. Dad had left ravioli and Black Forest gateau – one of my favourites! – for dinner, and I ate quite a lot of that because Petal only wanted salad and Pip won't eat ravioli on account of the sauce being red, so he just had a tin of sardines, which he disgustingly ate straight out of the tin, then went rushing off to do his homework.

Round about nine o'clock I had a bit of a sinking feeling and nibbled some biscuits, but by the time I went to bed I was feeling really miserable. I do try very hard not to be oversensitive, like there's this girl at school, Winona Pye (I know she can't help her name) who just starts crying at the least little thing. I find that quite annoying. But it is horrid to be told that you are fat! Especially in front of all your classmates. It is really hurtful. I don't care how much people go on about not being ashamed of your body, and saying how we can't all look like fashion models, and that in any case why should we want to? They can go on all they like, it's still horrid! 'Cos the truth is that nobody, practically, I shouldn't think, actually *enjoys* being fat.

That was the night I made my big decision: from now on I was going to stop behaving like the human equivalent of a dustbin. I was going to slim!

six

ALL THIS HAPPENED at the end of term. I made up my mind that when we went back after the break I would be slim as a pin. Well, perhaps not quite that slim. If I starved for an entire month I didn't think, probably, that I could get to be *that* slim. Maybe as slim as a darning needle. But at least a size smaller than I was now! All my clothes would be loose, so that I would have to buy a whole load of new ones. That was OK. I would ask Dad if I could take my savings money out of the building society, and Dad, in his Daddish way, would say, "Oh, you don't want to do that! You can go into Marshall's and use the store card."

I wouldn't ask Mum because Mum was harder than Dad. She was more likely to say that I didn't need new clothes, I'd just had new clothes. Which was true! We'd gone into Marshall's just before Christmas. Only then I'd been *plump* and now I was going to be *thin*. Now I could enjoy the experience! I would choose all the tightest, brightest, funkiest clothes that I could find. I would wear crop tops! I would wear skirts that showed my knickers! I would wear everything that I'd never been able to wear before.

Well, that was the theory. Unfortunately, when you have spent twelve years of your life as a human dustbin, it is not very easy to break the habit. Being holiday time just made it worse! I didn't even have Saffy to help me, because she was away for two weeks visiting her gran. I went out a few times with a girl from our class at school called Ro Sullivan, who lives just a couple of streets away, but we are not all that close and it wasn't like being with Saffy. I couldn't tell Ro about my struggles!

Mostly I just stayed home and practised voice exercises and dreamt about how it would be when I was thin. Petal was out every day, screaming round town with her friends, and Pip spent most of the time at his computer club or round at his friend Daniel's, which meant that I was on my own with Dad. A fatal combination! For a would-be thin person, that is. Dad's day is punctuated at regular intervals by what he calls "snackypoos". Like every two hours he would cheerily sing out, "Pumpkin! Time for snackypoos!"

At first I tried to resist.

"I'm not hungry!" I would nobly cry (while in fact being *starving,* having done my best not to eat any breakfast).

Alternatively, "I'm too busy!" "I'm working!" "I haven't got time!"

But Dad is not someone who will take no for an answer. Not where food is concerned. He'd knock on my bedroom door and when I opened it he'd be there, beaming, with a plate of macaroons that he'd just made, or a wodge of gorgeous sticky chocolate cake. I can't resist chocolate cake! Even more, I can't resist it when I know he's done it specially for me.

"Done it specially for you! Special treatie. Don't let me down!"

Before I knew it, we'd be cosily perched on the bed together, eating yummy chocolate cake. Two hours later it would be lunchtime. Then another snackypoo. Then

95

teatime at about half-past three, then dinner at five, before Dad left for work. Maybe even supper if I was still awake when he came back. We were fellow foodies! It was Us against Them. (Mum and Petal and Pip.) How could I disappoint him? If I went over to the other side, it would leave Dad on his own! How many times had he said to me "It's me and you, Pumpkin! Got to keep the flag flying."

Not that I can blame it all on Dad. I mean, he was just as used to me being a human waste disposal unit as I was. He wasn't to know that I'd become sickened by the sight of my own body. I did sort of try, in a half-hearted way, to tell him. One evening when Petal was out smooching with her latest boyfriend and Pip was round at Daniel's, and Dad and me were tucking into spaghetti bolognese together, I was overcome by this sudden burst of willpower and pushed my plate away from me. Dad was immediately concerned.

"What's the matter? Aren't you feeling well?"

He knew it wasn't his cooking. So it had to be me! I muttered that I was getting fat. Dad said, "Fat? Rubbish! Well-covered."

I said, "But I don't want to be well-covered!"

"Now, Pumpkin, don't be like that," said Dad. "You'll have me worried. We don't want any of that anorexic nonsense!"

I said, "It's not nonsense. This stuff is *fattening*."

"It's good for you," said Dad.

"It's not good to be fat," I said.

96

"You are *not fat*," said Dad. "You're my little plump Pumpkin and just the way you ought to be. You take after your dad, there's nothing you can do about it. Now eat your spaghetti and don't upset me!"

I didn't have to buy any new clothes. I didn't even have to take in any waistbands. I still couldn't roll them over, like Petal. I didn't dare step on the scales. By the time I went back to drama classes I was even plumper than I'd been before. I looked at all those cool thin people that first Friday of the new term and I hated myself worse than ever. I hated myself so much that I almost couldn't bear to change into my leotard and tights ready for our work-out session. I didn't want to be seen! I had a spare tyre, I wobbled when I walked. I felt like running away and hiding!

I really thought that I would have to tell Saffy I was going to give up. I would tell her that I wasn't going to come to classes any more. I would say that I was bored or that I wanted to do something else. Something such as... cooking. At cookery classes there would surely be other fatties; I wouldn't feel so grotesque.

Saturday morning I did this really cowardly thing: I rang Saffy and said that I wouldn't be going to class that afternoon as I wasn't feeling well. Saffy wailed at me.

"Jenn*ee*! You can't miss class!"

I wasn't brave enough to tell her that I wasn't ever going back to classes ever again. I just mumbled that I felt sick.

"I'd only throw up over everyone."

Saffy giggled and said that that was all right. "Just so long as you don't do it over me!"

She did her best to make me change my mind, but I wouldn't. I couldn't face it! Instead, I spent the day comfort eating. I had lots of snackypoos up in my room, where no one could see me. Dad has to work on a Saturday, so I snacked by myself. It wasn't as much fun, because snacking by yourself makes you feel really guilty, but I just had this great need. Every half hour or so I'd make these little furtive dashes downstairs to raid the fridge and go galloping back up with a chunk of pizza or a cream slice hidden under my sweater.

Mum was out, showing someone round a house, and Pip was shut away in his room. He always seemed to be shut in his room these days. I tried asking him once, what he did in there. I said, "I suppose you're playing with your computer?" He gave me this look of anguished scorn and said, "I don't *play*, I *work*." I said, "What, all the time?" "I have to!" said Pip. It really wasn't natural; not for a ten year old. But what could I do? I had far too much on my mind to worry about Pip and his sad way of life.

Then there was Petal, running all about the place like a mad woman with her mobile clamped to her ear, screaming at people.

"Don't tell me! Just don't tell me! I don't want to

know!" Followed almost immediately by, "What, what? Tell me!"

I put it down to boyfriend trouble. Everything with Petal comes back to boyfriends. No big deal. She'll get over it.

While I'm furtively helping myself to some lemon meringue pie from the fridge, Petal suddenly appears in the doorway, pale and distraught, looking like the mask of tragedy (as opposed to the mask of comedy) and I almost say "What's wrong?" but in the end I don't because I have enough problems of my own without frazzling my brain over hers. In any case, what problems can you possibly have when you're as thin and as pretty as she is? It's sheer self-indulgence. I'm the one with problems!

We pass each other several times as Petal distractedly rushes to and fro and I creep in and out of the kitchen on my secret missions, but we never exchange any words. Petal never asks me *why* I keep racing up and down the stairs, and in and out the kitchen. I never ask her *why* she looks like the end of the world is about to come upon us. And neither of us spares a thought for our little genius brother, behind his bedroom door. We are all locked into our separate lives.

When Mum got back at lunchtime she was expecting to take me to drama classes, as usual. I couldn't very well tell her that I was feeling sick or she'd have started fussing – well, no, actually she wouldn't, Mum is not the sort of person to fuss. But she might have made me eat something really boring when we went up to Giorgio's for a meal later on. Something like a boiled egg, for instance. Or just a plate of soup and nothing else. I didn't want that! So I just said that I didn't think I could be bothered with drama any more, and Mum said that was a pity as I'd seemed to be enjoying it, but she didn't press me. She didn't even point out that she and Dad had paid for a term's classes and would have wasted their money.

But I think she was quite pleased that she didn't have to fetch and carry because she said, "Well, if you're sure... I might as well pop back to the office for a couple of hours. I've got some stuff I need to clear up. Will you be all right here by yourself?"

I told her that I would, and she went off quite happily, leaving Pip in his bedroom and me in mine and Petal still clamped to her mobile. Whatever Petal's (purely imaginary) problems were she obviously got the better of them because when I crept downstairs for my next bout of comfort eating I found her all dressed up and about to leave the house. I heard her cooing, in syrupy tones, into her mobile, that she was "on her wayeee!" She would never speak like that to any of her girlfriends so I guessed she was off to make it up with her latest gorgeous guy and do whatever it was they did together. Smooch and slurp round the shopping centre, guzzle each other's lips in the back row of the cinema. Disgusting, really. But nowhere near as disgusting as me, with all my flab and my wobbly thighs. I thought self-pityingly that I was probably just jealous, because what boy would ever want to smooch and slurp with a great fat pumpkin?

I expect by now you will be thinking to yourself, what is the matter with this girl? Why doesn't she just stop shovelling food down her throat if it bothers her so much, being fat? All I can say is this: it is easier said than done. For starters, you don't always notice that you're getting fat until it's too late. You've already got there! You can see these huge unsightly bulges ballooning out all over, out of your waistband, out of your sleeves, and it is so utterly depressing that the only thing to bring you any solace is... FOOD. But not just any food! Not fruit or muesli bars or sticks of raw carrot. Fruit and muesli bars and raw carrot don't bring any solace at all. It has to be chips or crisps or slices of pizza. Cheesecake or chocolate or Black Forest gateau. So you eat because you hate yourself and then you hate yourself even more so then you have to eat even more, and you just get fatter and fatter and fatter.

Well, that is what *can* happen. It is what probably would have happened if Saffy hadn't rung me at five o'clock that evening, when she got back from class.

"Hey! Jen!" she cried. "Guess what?"

I said, "What?" Thinking rather meanly to myself that if it was something nice for Saffy then I didn't want to hear about it. I was that low.

"Are you sitting down?" said Saffy.

"No," I said. "I'm standing up. Why?"

"'Cos I don't want you throwing a wobbly! Just make sure you're holding on to something... D'you remember that person that came in? That publishing person? Last term?"

I said, "Mm."

"D'you remember she was looking for faces? For this book they were doing?"

I said, "Mm," thinking *please don't say they've chosen Saffy! PLEASE!* I know it was horrid of me, but that is the way it gets you when you are depressed.

"Well." Saffy paused. (Dramatic effect. We'd practised it on Friday.) "She wants *you*!"

I said, "M-me?"

"Yes! You!"

I said, "W-what for?"

"To be this girl on the cover of the book! It's called *Here Comes Ellen* and you're going to be Ellen!"

I gulped. I couldn't believe it! I just couldn't believe that anyone would want *me*.

"H-how do you know?" I said.

"'Cos Mrs Ambrose asked me where you were. She wanted to tell you... they want to take your photo! She's going to ring," said Saffy, "and talk to your mum." She added that the Terrible Two had gone "green as gooseberries" when they heard.

"They really thought it was going to be one of them!"

I'd have thought so, too. Anyone would have thought so! Who'd want me rather than Twinkle or Zoë?

"Your face will be all over," said Saffy. "You'll be famous!"

I zoomed up out of my depression so fast it was like a space rocket taking off. One minute I was practically grovelling on the ground, the next it was like zing, zap, pow! Up to the ceiling!

I told Mum about it as soon as she got in. I told Petal and Pip. I told Dad when we went up to Giorgio's. Dad told Giorgio and Giorgio made this big announcement in the middle of the restaurant! Lots of the customers were regulars, who knew us. They all wrote down the name of the book and promised to buy it when it was published.

Next day, Dad rang up both my grans and told them, and then he told my aunties and uncles, and then he rushed round to tell the next-door neighbours. He was so proud! I think he told almost the whole road. Even Mum was excited. She said she was going to tell everyone at the office.

"I'll get them all to buy copies!"

Everyone was going to buy copies. Even people at school. I wouldn't have said anything to people at school as it would have sounded too much like boasting, but Saffy insisted. She said, "Jen, you're a *star*. You're going to be famous!"

She told Dani Morris and Sophie Sutton. She told Ro Sullivan. She even told our class teacher, Mrs Carlisle, who said, "Oh! We'll have to make sure we get copies for the school library." Soon it seemed that everybody knew. I was a celeb!

On Friday when I went back to class – I didn't care so much now about being plump. Not now that I'd been chosen for a book jacket! – a photographer came to take pictures of me. The lady from the publishers was with him. She told me that Ellen was "very lovable and cuddly and *pretty*. You're exactly right!"

I knew I mustn't let it go to my head, because I really despise people who gloat and smirk and think they're

better than anyone else, but it was hard not to be just a little bit exultant as I was led away to have my photo taken. The look on Zoë's face! You could tell that she was thinking, "Why her? Why not me?"

And it wasn't just honour and glory! They were going to *pay* me for it. It was my first professional engagement! Saffy said that I was "on the way". She said, "Sucks to Deirdre Dobson! Sour old bag. I told you she was talking rubbish!"

Now that I wasn't depressed any more, I didn't have to comfort eat. But now that I'd been chosen for a book jacket I decided that I didn't have to go on any stupid diet, either. I wasn't fat! I was cuddly. And *pretty*. Just

105

like Ellen! So I stopped raiding the fridge but I went on having snackypoos with Dad and generally mopping up all the stuff that other people didn't want, and I sort of closed my eyes to the spare tyre and the wobbly thighs. You can do this, if you really try. I mean, you don't *have* to keep looking at yourself in the mirror. Not the whole of yourself. You can just concentrate on selected bits and forget about the rest. Which is what I learnt to do.

And then one day, a few weeks later, a padded envelope came through the letter box. It was addressed to me, and inside was an early copy of *Here Comes Ellen*. And there was my face on the front of it! Mum and Dad, and even Petal, said that it was lovely. And it was quite nice, though it wasn't the nicest one they'd taken. It was a bit... well! A bit sort of... not very bright-looking. At least, that's the way it seemed to me. Mum and Dad said "Nonsense!" but Petal, after studying the picture from all angles, said she could see what I meant.

"Like she's one slice short of a sandwich."

Mum said, "Petal! Don't be so unkind."

"She said it first," said Petal. "I'm only agreeing with her!"

I raced upstairs to my bedroom and settled down to read about this girl Ellen. This girl that was so lovable and cuddly and *pretty*. I discovered that Ellen was a Fat Girl. She was also a Slow Girl. A girl with learning difficulties. A girl that's bullied and jeered at. A figure of fun!

106

That was why I'd been chosen. Because I was *fat*. And when the book was published and was in the shops everyone, but everyone, would be rushing out to buy it, and people like my grans would be feeling just *so* sorry for me, poor little Jenny! What a horrid thing to do to her! Whereas people like Zoë and Twink and Dani Morris would be laughing themselves silly.

I didn't finish reading the book. I couldn't bear to. Saffy told me ages later that in fact Ellen turned out to be a heroine, but it still didn't stop her being *fat*. I didn't want to know! I got half way through and then hid the hateful thing at the back of a cupboard. If Mum or Dad asked me about it, I would say I'd lent it to someone and they'd lost it. I didn't want them reading it! I didn't want anyone reading it.

You might think that at this point, being such a pathetic sort of person, I would have instantly fallen into another depression and rushed downstairs to fetch myself a snackypoo. But I didn't! I am not always pathetic. Sometimes I bounce. I get defiant. I think to myself that I will show them!

That is what I thought that evening in my bedroom. I made a vow: by the end of term, when we filmed *Sob Story* and I did my transformation scene, I was no longer going to be a fat girl. I was going to be a thin girl!

This time, *I meant it*.

seven

THIS IS WHEN I became obsessed. It is very easy to become obsessed. It is a question of focusing all your energies on just one thing and sticking to it. The thing that I was focusing on was the size of my body. Big fat bloated pumpkin! The fat was going to *go*.

I didn't tell anyone; not even Saffy. It was a matter of pride. I didn't want people knowing how much I cared. It was too pathetic! When I got thin, I wanted them to think it was just something that had happened quite naturally, all on its own, without any help from me.

"Jen!" they would go. "You've lost weight!"

And I would go, "Really? I hadn't noticed."

Like just so-o-o cool. I would be able to be cool once I was thin. It's difficult to be cool when you're fat. It's difficult to be *anything* when you're fat. You can't ever look good. You just go round hating yourself and trying not to catch sight of your reflection in shop windows. It does terrible things to your confidence. Well, you just don't really have any.

But that was all going to change! I started counting calories. I read the information on the backs of packets.

Per pie... 350 calories.

BAD.

Per half can... 210 calories.

BAD.

Per slice... 400 calories.

Bad, bad, VERY BAD!

I soon discovered that there was almost nothing in the house that I could safely consume. I looked up pizza and pasta and chocolate fudge cake in a book that I bought called *Calorie Counter*. They were all *bad*. Chocolate fudge cake was deadly! In fact, most of my favourite foods fell into the same category.

B.A.D.

FATTENING!

All the nicest foods are. It is a sad fact of life.

So far as I could, I simply stopped eating. I weighed myself on the bathroom scales every morning when I got up and every night before I went to bed. It became a sort of ritual. My life revolved around the bathroom scales! If I found that I'd put on even so much as .1 of a kilo, it nagged at me all day, it kept me awake all night. Even if I just stayed the same, it threw me into total despair. Usually, for some weird reason, I weighed less in the morning than I did in the evening. I couldn't understand that, when all I'd done all night was sleep. How could you lose weight just sleeping? I thought that if I could stay in bed for a whole month without eating I would be thin as a thread without any trouble  at all! But even Mum would notice if I took to my bed. She didn't notice me not eating because she either wasn't there or was in too much of a rush.

Dad was my really *big* problem. Pip and Petal were like Mum, too bound up in their own affairs. Just as my life revolved round the bathroom scales, Pip's revolved round homework and his computer, Petal's revolved round boyfriends. They wouldn't notice if I lived on nothing but air and water.

But Dad would! Dad has eyes like a hawk where food is concerned. So what I had to do, I had to devise strategies. Being on a really determined slimming spree can make you very cunning. I would let Dad pile my plate as usual, then suddenly discover, at breakfast for example, that I was wearing the wrong shoes, or the wrong top, and go racing upstairs to change – *carrying my plate with me*. I would then dump the whole lot down the loo.

Or another strategy I had, I would pick and poke at my food, pretending to be eating it, then as soon as Dad left the kitchen I would dive across to the sink and scrape everything into the rubbish bin – being careful to cover it up with tea leaves or orange peel or whatever happened to be in the rubbish bin to start with. I told you I was cunning!

Once or twice, when I couldn't think of an excuse for going upstairs and Dad didn't leave the kitchen, I actually picked up my plate and wandered out into the garden with it. There's lots of porridge and pizza and ravioli hidden behind the bushes in our garden.

I did sometimes think of all those starving people around the globe and feel a twinge of guilt, but I comforted myself with the thought that if I wasn't chucking the stuff behind the rose bushes or dumping it down the loo, I would be eating it myself, so it still wouldn't get to the people who needed it. Such – alas! – is the way of the world. Too much food in one place, and not enough in another. You would think by now we could have arranged things a bit better. I, for instance, would have been only too happy to save up a week's supply and take it along to a central collecting point for redistribution. Far better than throwing it behind the rose bushes.

Fortunately, from my point of view, neither Mum nor Dad is into gardening, so they never came across the little festering piles of food. Probably the foxes mopped it up. Or the hedgehogs, or the squirrels. Or even next door's cat. But that was OK. If the starving people couldn't have it, I'd rather it went to the animals.

Weekends were the worst time. At weekends we always went up to Giorgio's and I couldn't very well keep rushing off to the loo with platefuls of pasta in the middle of a crowded restaurant. I thought even Mum might notice if I did that. One time when the weather was warm we sat at a table outside, on the pavement, and I toyed with the idea of upending my plate into a potted something-or-other, some kind of leafy thing, that stood nearby, but at the last minute I chickened out.

All I could do was try ordering the least fattening things I could find, but most of the stuff on Giorgio's menu is smothered in oil or butter or rich creamy sauce – *bad, bad, TRIPLE bad*! – and even if I just asked for soup and a sorbet the waiter would come beaming up with a dish of tiramisu or cheesecake, "with the chef's compliments". Mum would say, "Go on! Eat it. You've hardly touched a thing," and I knew if I sent it back Dad himself would come out and demand in hurt tones to know what was wrong. It was no use offering it to Mum because she would already have ordered her favourite, which was apple pie and cream, and it goes without saying that Petal wouldn't help me out.

"Ugh! I don't want it," she'd say, giving one of her little shudders.

So then I'd try Pip, but he'd just push it right back at me like it was something repulsive. Cold sick, or nose droppings. If Pip had a pudding it was always ice cream. *Green* ice cream. He says that white tastes like cardboard, and pink, of course, is too close to red. Likewise chocolate. I sometimes wonder if Pip is quite normal, but maybe geniuses aren't.

Mostly, at Giorgio's, I had to eat what I had always eaten, for fear of drawing attention to myself. I didn't want Mum to suss what was going on. I knew she would immediately think "Anorexia!" because that is what they always think. It is the modern bogey word for mums.

When we got back from Giorgio's I would always feel very ill and bloated. It was truly disgusting, eating so much! I knew I had to offload it, so I would wait until Mum was relaxing in front of the television then I would shut myself in the loo and stick my fingers down my throat and bring everything up. Not very nice, but it had to be done. In any case, I remembered reading somewhere how Princess Di had done the same thing. If she could do it, so could I! It had obviously worked for her, she had always looked so beautiful. I thought that I would give anything to look like Princess Di!

As well as jumping on and off the scales twice a day, I also took to measuring myself, specially round my waist and hips. I measured once when I got up, *before* I weighed myself; and once when I went to bed, *after* I'd weighed myself. This is what you do when you get obsessed. If I could have measured and weighed during the day as well, I would have done! I did at weekends. At weekends I practically lived on the scales.

At school I didn't really eat at all; it was easier there. I still had to go into the dining hall, but nobody checked what you had on your tray. I would just take a bit of salad and a yoghurt, and sit there nibbling at it while Saffy, as usual, tucked into chips and doughnuts and various other assorted goodies. *Baddies!* Saffy could eat an elephant and still look like a stick insect. Life is just not fair.

But then, whoever said it was? Certainly not me!

One lunchtime, when I was cutting up a lettuce leaf, Saffy said, "*Jen*! You're not *slimming*, are you?"

The way she said it, you'd have thought I was planning to rob a bank or mug a little kid for his mobile phone. I felt my face surge into the red zone. Slimming! Why did it sound so shameful? I might have known that Saffy would notice. We always notice things about each other. It's what comes of being so close.

"*Are* you?" she said. All grim and accusing.

I said, "Yes, I am, as a matter of fact."

"But why?" said Saffy.

Did she really need to ask? I would have thought it was obvious.

"I'm fat," I said. We were sitting by ourselves at the far end of a table so nobody could hear us. I wouldn't have said it otherwise. I would have been too ashamed.

"Jenny, are you mad?" shrieked Saffy.

Everyone turned to look, and I went, "Shh!"

"Well, but really," she hissed, "we've already been through this! You are *not fat*!"

"Look," I said, "it's my body. I ought to know whether it's fat or not."

"You're just being silly and oversensitive," said Saffy.

I muttered, "You'd be silly and oversensitive if you looked like me."

"I wouldn't mind looking like you," said Saffy.

I said, "Oh, no?"

"No! If you want to know the truth, I'd give anything to have hair like yours."

It is true that my hair is quite thick, while Saffy's is rather straggly. And her nose is decidedly pointy, and she is definitely not pretty. But she is *thin*.

"Honestly," said Saffy, "you're not fat, Jen! Really!"

"So what would you call it?" I said.

"I'd say you were... chubby."

"*Chubby?*"

"Cuddly!"

"Cuddly," I said, "is just another way of saying *fat*."

"Oh! Well." Saffy pushed her plate away from her. She had eaten chips and lentil bake. My stomach cried out in protest, and I rammed a lettuce leaf down my throat to keep it quiet. "If that's the way you want to think of yourself," said Saffy.

She sounded like she was just about fed up with me. Desperately, I said, "Saf, I *am* fat! I've got to do something about it."

"I thought we'd already been through all this?" said Saffy. "They'd hardly have chosen you for a book jacket if you were fat!"

So then I told her. I told her how lovable cuddly Ellen was a Fat Girl, and how I'd hidden the book at the back of my cupboard and didn't want anyone to read it.

That shook her, I could tell. I mean, that anyone could be so horrid! They had *tricked* me. Good as.

Then Saffy said slowly, "She may be fat in the book, but they wouldn't actually put anyone fat on the cover. Not *really* fat. That's why they chose you, because you're *not* really fat. You're cuddly!"

Saffy is such a good friend. She was really trying to cheer me up.

"With you on the cover," she said, "I should think it would go like hot cakes! Everyone will buy it!"

She wasn't to know that was just about the worst thing she could have said. I didn't want everyone to buy it! I didn't want anyone to buy it. I said this to Saffy. I said, "It's going to be published next week. It'll be in all the book shops. I just can't bear it!"

Our town has rather a lot of bookshops. There's Smith's, for a start. That's in the shopping centre. Then there is Waterstone's on the top floor, and Books Etc. in the High Street, and a tiny little place tucked away down the hill. Just imagine if they all had the book!

"Do your mum and dad know you're slimming?" said Saffy.

I said, "No! And you're not to tell them."

"I bet they wouldn't approve," said Saffy. "Specially your dad."

"It's nothing to do with them," I said. "It's my body!"

Saffy promised not to tell, but I could see she was dubious about the whole enterprise.

"So long as you don't overdo it," she said. "You know what happened to Pauline Pretty."

Pauline Pretty was a girl in Year 10 who'd faded away to practically nothing before anyone realised what was happening. There'd been an announcement last term in assembly, saying that she'd died. We'd all been shocked, even people such as me and Saffy who hadn't even known who she was. It was just the thought of someone our age, *dying*. But Pauline Pretty had had anorexia. She had been sick. I wasn't sick! I just wanted to get thin.

I said as much to Saffy and she said, "But then you won't be you!" I thought to myself that if being me meant being fat, then I didn't want to be me. I wanted to be someone different! Only I didn't say this to Saffy as I didn't want her to lecture me. Next week that hateful book would be in the bookshops and I needed Saffy to help me go round and hide it, because this was what I had decided to do. I couldn't stop it being sold in other places, but I was determined it wasn't going to be sold in my home town!

The following Saturday we met up in the shopping centre to go on a *Here Comes Ellen* hunt. We went all round the bookshops, starting with Smith's. The tiny little tucked-away place didn't have it, but all the others did. Waterstone's actually had it on a table! In full view of everyone!

"Oh, Jen, I don't know what you're going on about," said Saffy. "It looks brilliant! Why don't we just leave it?"

I said, "No! I don't want anyone buying it."

So when nobody was looking we took the books off the table and scattered them round the shelves, putting them behind other books that were face out. We did the same in Books Etc. and in Smith's. In Smith's the book *itself* was face out, and that was really frightening because loads of people go into Smith's. I mean, people that want other things, like CDs and stationery, and I had visions of them strolling past the book section and suddenly catching sight of my face staring at them from the cover and going, "Oh! That's that girl whose dad works in Giorgio's!" or "Oh, that's that girl that goes to my school!" So I took some of the books that were next

119

to it and turned *them* face out and stuck *Ellen* behind them and hoped she would stay there, hidden from view, until she grew old and musty and the shop sent her back where she came from. And serve her right!

Saffy wondered about the poor author. She said how upset she would be when nobody bought any of her books, but I said that I didn't care.

"It was mean of them not to tell me!"

"Well, anyway, it's probably selling like mad everywhere else," said Saffy.

I know Saffy means well, but there are times when she can be just *so* tactless.

eight

LOSING WEIGHT IS a bit like saving money: it is very difficult to get going. You find that you are making all kinds of excuses such as, "I'll just finish this last packet of Maltesers, I'll just wait till my birthday, I'll just wait till after the weekend." etc. and so forth. And then, sometimes, you never get started at all, which was what had happened to me when I first decided to slim. I put it off so long, and had so many snackypoos and bars of chocolate, that in the end it didn't seem worth the effort. But once you *do* manage to get started it's like your life becomes ruled by it. You can't imagine living any other way. It gets so it's impossible to stop. Both with losing weight and with saving money.

Like there was this one time I remember, in Year 6, when I desperately, desperately wanted a personal organiser like a girl in my class had got. I didn't know what I was going to do with it; I just knew that I had to have one! Dad would have let me, but Mum as usual was more stern. She said I'd just spent all my Christmas money on what she called "useless rubbish" (meaning bangles and earrings and sparkly hair clips, which may be useless rubbish to Mum but certainly isn't to me!) and if I wanted a personal organiser as badly as all that I could save up for it. I wailed that it would take me ages.

"I'll be dead by the time I've saved up that much!"

So then Mum relented and said all right, if I could manage to save half she and Dad would come up with the other half. So I started to save, just little bits to begin with like the odd 20p, because I don't have very much pocket money, well I don't think I do, and I kept it in a jam jar with a plastic lid so that I could see how quickly it was mounting up. At first it didn't seem to mount up at all, but then one day I suddenly noticed that the jam jar was almost quarter full, and I took out the money and counted it and it came to nearly £6. Six pounds that I had saved almost without realising it!

That was when it got a grip and I started to save in real earnest. I saved every penny that I could! I even picked up 1p pieces that people had dropped in the street. When the first jam jar was full, I started on a second one. By the time the second one was full I'd saved my half of the money and could have had my organiser any time I wanted, but now I didn't want one. Well, I did, but I wanted the money more. I didn't want to *do* anything with the money; I just wanted to see it mounting up. I had become a money junkie! I was a secret hoarder!

I might have been hoarding to this day if something hadn't happened to break the cycle. It was only a little something, but that is often all it takes. Quite suddenly, for no reason, the whole of Year 6 went mad on body tattoos – the sort you stick on. If you didn't walk round covered in them, you just weren't cool. I begged Saffy to give me some of hers, but she wouldn't. She said I'd become as mean as could be and could go out and buy some of my own. So I did, and that was the beginning of the end. We went to visit my auntie and uncle and they took us to the shopping centre at Brent Cross and I saw these really *superior* tattoos in a shop and I just couldn't resist them, even though they were expensive.

I knew if I went to school with tattoos like that I'd be the coolest person there. I spent the whole of my pocket money on body tattoos! And that was that. Once I'd broken the habit, I couldn't get back into it again. I didn't even get the personal organiser; I just frittered the money away on more of what Mum called "rubbish".

So this is how it was with me and slimming, except that instead of money mounting up, it was kilos going *down*. I bought a red felt tip, a fine liner, and used it to mark the tape measure. Every time I measured myself, I made a little mark. At first, just as with the money in the jam jar, nothing very much seemed to be happening and it would have been all too easy to be discouraged, except that this time I was *determined*. And then, suddenly, the red mark moved! In the right direction, I hasten to add. Week by week, it kept on moving. Just a millimetre at a time, to begin with, then one Saturday a whole half centimetre! I could hardly contain myself! I immediately tried on every single skirt and pair of jeans in my wardrobe and discovered to my joy that some of them that I'd had difficulty fitting into now did up quite easily. It was working! I was getting thin!

There came a day when I actually had to use a safety pin to take in the waistband of my school skirt and pull in the belt on my jeans really tight to stop them slipping down. It just felt *so good*. Zoë looked at me in the changing room one Friday, as we were getting into our leotards. She did this double take and said, "Hey! Eleflump!" which was what she had taken to calling me. "Are you on a diet, or something?"

As carelessly as I could I said, "Me? No! Why?" Hoping and praying that Saffy wouldn't give me away.

"You look like you are," said Zoë.

"Yes. You do!" Twinkle was now gazing at me. "You look sort of... thinner."

"Really?" I said. Yawn yawn.

"You used to *bulge*," said Twinkle. "You used to look like a big hovercraft." And she puffed out her cheeks and went waddling across the room with her feet splayed and her bottom stuck in the air and her arms held out like panniers.

"Flomp flomp flomp," went Zoë, joining in.

Such sweet girls. *Not*.

"You do look as if you've lost weight," said Portia.

I was pleased, of course, but also a bit embarrassed. I wanted people to notice – but I didn't want them remarking on it! Saffy was really good. She could easily have betrayed me, but she didn't. When Portia turned to her and said, "Don't you think she looks as if she's lost weight?" Saffy just said, "I suppose she does. I hadn't

125

really thought about it." But next day, when we went back to her place after class, she read me this mumsy-type lecture, all about how I'd lost as much weight as I needed and how I'd got to start eating properly.

"I can say this," she said, "'cos you're my friend. If you carry on not eating you'll get ill. You'll get hag-like. You'll end up like Pauline Pretty!"

What did she mean, I would end up like Pauline Pretty? How dare she say such a thing! I wasn't anorexic. I could stop any time I wanted, just like that! I said so to Saffy. I told her that I could stop *any time I wanted*.

"So when are you going to?" said Saffy.

I said, "As soon as I've reached my target weight."

"Which is what?"

Blusteringly I said, "Well! Whatever I decide."

I couldn't give her an exact weight because I didn't have one. I didn't have a target weight! I just had this fixed idea that I would go on slimming until I could finally look in the mirror and like what I saw. It wasn't a question of weight. It was a question of how I looked.

"I wish we'd never started drama classes if this is what it's done to you!" cried Saffy.

I said, "It was you that wanted to. Don't blame me!"

"I'm not blaming you," said Saffy.

"Sounds like you are."

"I'm not, but ever since that stupid woman came you've got all miserable and cranky and obsessed with yourself!"

"I'm just thinking of my future," I said. "If you don't mind! I'm just exercising a bit of *willpower*. You'd think," I said, "being my *friend*, you'd want to help me. Not go nagging on at me the whole time!"

Saffy pursed her lips, making them go into a narrow line. "What about your mum and dad?" she said.

I said, "What about them?"

"What do they say?"

"They don't say anything. *They* don't nag!"

The truth was that Mum and Dad still hadn't noticed. I was being that cunning! Plus Dad isn't the most observant of people, except when it's food. Plus Mum was always working. But I was developing new strategies all the time. I'd not only learnt how to avoid eating but when I was at home I'd deliberately wear clothes that made me look the same plump Pumpkin that I'd always been. I'd wear long baggy T-shirts over big saggy jeans, and when I dressed for school I'd wear my blouse outside my skirt. As soon as I left the house I'd tuck it back in and pin up the waistband. I didn't want to go out and buy new clothes until I'd reached my target body image.

That's what I was calling it. *Target body image.* I think I knew, deep down, that Saffy was right. I had to have some aim in view; I couldn't just keep slimming indefinitely. It was a question of knowing when to stop. And the answer to that was... when I was thin as a pin!

Sometimes on a Sunday me and Dad and Pip, and Petal if she doesn't have anything else to do, go and visit my gran. That is, Dad's mum. (The one I sort of based my old cranky person on for *Sob Story*, though as I believe I said before, my gran isn't really cranky. She just reckons that life is not as good now as it used to be when she was young.) Mum doesn't very often come with us when we visit as she and Gran don't get on awfully well, mainly because Gran thinks a mother's place is in the home. She thinks it is terrible that it was Dad who looked after us while Mum went out to work. So Mum usually stays behind while the rest of us go off, which is just as well for me since otherwise, on this particular occasion that we went to visit, I might have been found out!

Gran has very sharp eyes for an old lady; she notices things. She noticed *immediately* that I wasn't looking as gross as I had been.

"Jenny," she said. "Have you lost weight?"

Fortunately, although we were all together in the kitchen, Dad was busy checking the contents of Gran's cupboard – he always checks the cupboard, to make sure she's properly stocked up with food – and when Dad is counting tins of baked beans or jars of marmalade the rest of the world simply passes him by. If Mum had been there, she would have pounced! Even Petal might have looked twice, but she'd gone to spend the day with Helen Bickerstaff, one of her friends from school, and Pip didn't because what did he care if I'd lost weight?

"Well," said Gran. Like in these accusing tones. "*Have* you?"

I said, "I wish!" Flapping my hands in my T-shirt.

Gran said, "What do you mean, *you wish*? What kind of foolish talk is that?"

"Gran! Everybody wants to be slim," I said.

"Well, everybody shouldn't," said Gran. "Everybody should have a bit more sense. We're human beings, not stick insects!"

Dad then turned round from the cupboards to ask why Gran didn't have any pasta in stock, and the talk swung off in another direction, but I noticed Gran looking at me every now and again with narrowed eyes so I made sure to really *glut* when it came to teatime. I knew I'd have to pay for it later, but the last thing I wanted was Gran going and putting ideas into Dad's head. As we left she said in a loud voice, as she kissed me goodbye, "And no more of that *I wish* nonsense, thank you very much!" This time, Dad heard.

"What was that about?" he said.

I was about to say "Nothing," in a vague and meaningless kind of way, when Pip had to go and pipe up.

"She wants to be slim!"

I could willingly have strangled him. But Dad just said, "Oh! Is that all?" Obviously not taking it seriously. Phew! Relief. It did set me thinking, though. I thought, what is the point of losing all this weight if I still have to go round pretending to be fat in front of Mum and Dad? I decided that as soon as I had reached my target body image I would REVEAL ALL. By then I wouldn't need to diet any more, so it wouldn't matter what they said. After all, not even Dad could *force* me to eat pizzas and pasta and Black Forest gateau.

One Saturday – the Saturday after our visit to Gran – Mrs Ambrose announced that we were going to do some improvisation. She said that we could improvise on our own or with a partner, whichever we preferred, and the theme was to be "travelling".

She said, "You might be on a bus or a train... you might be walking, driving a car... riding a horse. You might be on a plane, you might be at an airport. Anything that takes your fancy! All go away and think about it, then we'll see what you've come up with."

Normally, me and Saffy would have been partners, but today, for some reason, she didn't seem to want to work with me. She teamed up with Portia instead. I thought, *Huh! See if I care.* I'd do it by myself.

I was just going off into a corner to think of something when Ben Azariah (whose hair grew to a point like a turnip) poked me in the ribs and said,

AMBROSE

"Hey, Jenny! Want to do it together?"

I frowned. I'd had this feeling, just recently, that Ben was getting a bit interested in me. Last term I might have been flattered. I mean, what with being so fat and not having much confidence. But I wasn't fat any more! I wasn't yet *thin*, but at least I wasn't bursting out of my clothes. I felt that now I could pick and choose. And I wasn't going to choose a geeky turnip head!

"No," I said. "I don't think so."

Ben's face fell. Just for a moment I felt sorry for him and wished I'd been nicer, but then I hardened my heart. People like Zoë and Twinkle didn't worry about being nice. It didn't bother them if they hurt someone's feelings. And *they* didn't get partnered by geeky turnip heads. Zoë had gone into a huddle with Gareth. Now if *he* had asked me...

"I thought we could do something funny," said Ben.

I didn't want to do anything funny! I was sick of being a figure of fun. I wanted to be a figure of romance!

131

"Sorry," I said. "I've got other ideas."

I swished off towards my chosen corner. Ben came scuttling after me. Some people just won't take no for an answer.

"It doesn't have to be funny," he said. "It can be anything you like!"

Not with a turnip head. How could you be romantic with a boy whose hair grew to a point? It looked ridiculous! Why didn't he have it cut?

"I want to do something by myself," I said.

I worked out this scene where I was on the Eurostar, travelling to Paris to meet my boyfriend. I was on my mobile, talking to him. Talking the language of love. When all of a sudden—

"We're going to crash!"

It was just so dramatic, and so sad. I really didn't know what people found to laugh at. There is nothing remotely amusing about a train crash.

Mrs Ambrose (mopping her eyes) said, "Jenny, I'm sorry! That was such a good idea. You weren't quite able to carry it off... but it was a brave attempt. Well done!"

Saffy said later the reason people had laughed was that one minute I'd sounded "all syrupy and slurpy" and then it was "Help, help! We're going to die!"

I said, "You must have a very warped sense of humour if you think that's funny."

"It was you that was funny," said Saffy.

Angrily I said, "You're sick! You know that? You are *sick*!"

"You're the one that's sick," said Saffy.

We parted on very bad terms. I didn't like quarrelling with Saffy, but just lately she had been really starting to annoy me. What had come over her? Why did she have to be so picky all the time?

I decided that I would ignore Saffy and concentrate on what I was going to wear for my transformation scene. Everyone knew that I was going to do a transformation scene, because I had introduced it at the last rehearsal; but nobody knew what I was going to wear! Neither did I. *Yet*.

I lay awake in bed that night, mentally trying on everything in my wardrobe and rejecting it all as too big,

too baggy, too boring. I'd got to look glam! But not what Mum would call "tarted up". I wasn't aiming for a fairy-at-the-top-of-the-Christmas-tree effect. I wanted to look more natural and casual, like I hadn't made any special kind of effort; but at the same time I wanted everyone to think "*Wow*." A difficult combination!

I knew what I was going to wear as an old lady: an ancient raincoat of Mum's that came down to my feet, with a scarf tied under the chin and a pair of joke specs with a long rubbery nose that had what looked like a dribble at the end. Truly disgusting! I'd found the specs in the Party Shop last time I'd gone to the shopping centre with Saffy.

The old lady gear was easy. But I spent the whole of Sunday morning desperately trying on clothes. They were just as baggy and boring as I'd feared! How could I ever have worn such stuff? Huge pairs of elephant trousers, and tops like tents. Ugh! It made me feel sick, just thinking of how I used to be. I still wasn't thin enough, nowhere near. I could still pinch bits of flesh between my fingers, and my thighs still went flomp! like jellies when I sat down. I had a good long way to go before I even approached my target body image, but at least I could now walk down the street without feeling that everyone was looking at me and going, "That is some fat girl!"

In the end, squashed away at the back of the wardrobe, I found a denim skirt that I hadn't been able to get into for absolutely ages. I'd forgotten all about it. I pulled it out and put it on, and oh, joy! It fitted me. I could see why I'd bought it. It had little embroidered stars on the pockets and a zip with a red tassel. And it was *short*! Really no more than a strip, 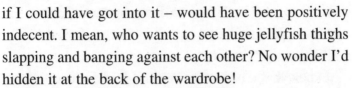 which if I'd worn it a few months ago – if I could have got into it – would have been positively indecent. I mean, who wants to see huge jellyfish thighs slapping and banging against each other? No wonder I'd hidden it at the back of the wardrobe!

What I needed now was a hot top to go with it, and maybe a pair of boots. I decided to ask Dad. Not Mum! I can wheedle almost anything out of Dad if I put my mind to it. I waited till I came home from school on Monday, when I could be sure of having him to myself. Dad was making a cheese sauce to go with some macaroni. He was eager for me to try it, so I obediently took a spoonful over to the sink and said, "Yum yum! That's good!" at the same time frantically running the tap and washing the sauce down the plug hole, because cheese is *extremely* fattening.

"Dad, do you think I could have a new top and a pair of boots?" I said. "I need them, Dad! It's for this show we're doing. We're going to film it on Saturday, and I've got nothing to wear!"

That was all the wheedling I needed to do. Dad was so taken up with his sauce that I think he would have said yes to anything. He told me to go ahead and buy whatever I needed.

"When do you want it?"

I said, "Tomorrow?"

"I'll come and pick you up after school," said Dad.

I was so grateful that I gave him a big hug and took another spoonful of sauce to dump in the sink.

"Is it OK?" said Dad.

"Scrummy!" I said.

I knew that it had to be, because Dad's sauces always are; and in any case some had touched my lips so that I'd been *almost* tempted to eat it. But I knew that I mustn't! Just one mouthful would be enough to set me right back. It had to be all or nothing – which was what I explained to Saffy when I invited her to join me on my shopping trip and she started on at me yet again about not eating.

"I don't know how your mum and dad let you get away with it. My mum would go spare if I stopped eating!"

"Look, just *shut up*," I said. I'd invited her to come with us 'cos I thought she'd enjoy it, helping me choose what to buy. Now she was going and ruining it all! "Don't keep on," I said. "It's very bad manners." I mean, for goodness' sake! She was my *guest*.

Dad took us to Marshall's and sat himself down in

a chair while me and Saffy roamed about, examining stuff. I could buy anything I wanted! Skinny rib, halter neck. Anything! With Saffy's help I finally got a blue T-shirt with writing on it (*Funky Babe*, in gold letters) plus a pair of blue denim boots with zips and high heels. I thought that Mum's raincoat would cover the heels so that no one would know I was wearing funky footgear and not old lady shoes. I swore Saffy to silence.

"You're not to tell anyone! It's got to be a surprise."

Saffy said, "Yeah. OK." and waved a hand like all of a sudden she was bored.

"Now what's the matter?" I said.

"You!" said Saffy. "Always giving orders. You're so *bossy*."

Well! Bossy is just about the last thing I am. I said, "Look who's talking! I'm not the one that's been going on."

At that point we left the changing room area and found ourselves back out in the open. Just as well, or we might seriously have fallen out. With Dad there we couldn't very well go on slinging accusations at each other so we both simmered down and tried to make like there was nothing wrong. Dad wanted to take us upstairs to the restaurant to have tea. Once I would have thought this was a brilliant idea, since Marshall's is famous for its cream cakes and squidgy buns. Once I would have guzzled a whole plateful of them. Today I was thrown into panic at the mere thought of it.

"Don't you think we ought to get home?" I said.

"No, I think we ought to go and have some tea," said Dad.

"But Saffy's got to get home!" I said. "Her mum will be wondering where she is."

"No, she won't," said Saffy. "I rang her."

"So what do you reckon?" said Dad. Talking to Saffy. Not *me*. "Do you reckon we ought to go and have some tea?"

"Yes, please!" beamed Saffy.

Oh! She was *such* a traitor. I glared at her all the way up in the lift, but she resolutely took no notice and chattered brightly to Dad about absolutely nothing.

"Now, what shall we have?" said Dad, rubbing

his hands in delighted anticipation as he studied the menu, which I am here to tell you is a total nightmare of carbohydrates and calories. "Mm... raspberry pavlova! How about that?"

Dad had raspberry pavlova, Saffy had fudge cake, I had the plainest thing I could find, which was a packet of boring biscuits. But even boring biscuits are fattening! If I'd been on my own with Dad I could have slid them off the table, one by one, and hidden them in my school bag. I couldn't do that with Saffy there; she watched me the whole time. Well, actually, she watched the biscuits. She got, like, fixated on them. I just had this feeling that if I tried anything she would tell on me. So I had to force myself to eat them. It nearly made me gag! There is nothing worse than having to eat when you don't want to.

But anyway, ho ho to Saffy! The minute I got home I did my usual trick. I raced upstairs to the lavatory and stuck my fingers down my throat. I was distinctly annoyed with Saffy, though, because it is not at all pleasant sticking your fingers down your throat. For one thing it makes your throat sore, and for another it makes your stomach muscles ache with all the heaving and straining you have to do. But I couldn't afford to put on weight. I had to be thin for my transformation scene!

nine

SATURDAY CAME. AND I was so excited! We all were, but me, I think, more than anyone. I put on my transformation outfit before leaving home, with Mum's raincoat over the top. I wanted it to stay a secret right until the very end! While everyone else was changing, I sat in a corner, huddled in my raincoat with all the buttons done up. People kept tweaking at it and going, "Come on! Let's see what you're wearing!" but I wouldn't let them.

"I bet *she* knows," said Twinkle, pointing at Saffy. "Tell, tell! What's she got on?"

"My lips are sealed," said Saffy, zipping a finger across her mouth.

One girl, Mitch Bosworth, even crawled on her hands and knees and tried to see underneath! The boys were nowhere near as interested. In fact, they didn't really seem to care what I had on underneath Mum's raincoat. I thought that was good, because then it would really come as a surprise.

Filming was due to start at two o'clock. I had always thought that making films was a very slo-o-o-w and laborious process. I'd read somewhere that it could take an entire day just to shoot one tiny little scene, but we filmed the whole of *Sob Story* in one afternoon. I suppose it wasn't quite the same as real movie-making. Two students came in from the local art college with a video camera and we just had one final run-through and then it was, like, *go for it*!

We did have one or two stops and starts. That silly girl Mitch Bosworth, for instance, got the giggles, and Saffy went and forgot her lines. Her *own* lines, that she had made up. She just, like, froze, and this trapped expression appeared on her face. It wasn't quite as bad as the angel disaster back in Juniors, when she had to be led off stage, sobbing; but I did think it went to show that she was not cut out to be an actress.

Zoë, on the other hand, far from forgetting her lines actually went and added to them! She launched into this mad speech that she had *never* done before. It went on and on, going absolutely nowhere, saying absolutely nothing, and the rest of us just standing around with our mouths sagging open, wondering what to do. It was Mark who saved the day. He just suddenly cut in over the top of her, and that shut her up. If it hadn't been for him, she might have gone rambling on for ever, and all the things that were supposed to happen – all the things that we had so carefully rehearsed – would no longer have made any sense. Mark pulled it all together again, and I thought that showed that he was a true pro. Whereas Zoë was nothing more than a silly selfish show-off, with no control over her own mouth.

I would like to report that I *rose to the occasion*, as the saying goes. I would like to tell how I rushed in to the rescue, and came to Mark's support as he struggled to get us back on track; but I didn't! I wasn't a true pro. I just stood around with the rest of them, gaping, and not knowing what to do. I felt like running at Zoë and strangling her, but in fact I took root, like a pot plant, and did nothing at all. I was just so worried that she might ruin my transformation scene! That was all I cared about. I had long since lost any interest in being a crotchety old woman who went round complaining. I didn't care if it did make people laugh. I didn't want people to laugh! I wanted them to gasp and go *wow*! I wanted to be glamorous! I wanted Gorgeous Gareth to be gobsmacked! I wanted Beautiful Mark to take notice of me... which I suppose must mean that I am no more cut out to be an actress than Saffy. *Sigh*.

Thanks to Mark and his quick thinking, we were able to move on. We got to the end. My big moment... ba-boom! Gasp. Wow!!!

Nobody actually did gasp or go "wow!" because by now they were all expecting it, and in any case it would have been unprofessional, but Zoë came up to me in the changing room afterwards and said, "Great get up, Gran!" Portia said I looked fab, and Mitch Bosworth told me that "That was a really neat idea... like  something out of panto." Only that stupid Twinkle had to go and upset me. She poked me in the ribs and said, "Come on, you can tell us now! You *have* been slimming, haven't you? Was it because of the book?"

Acting as hard as I could go, I said, "What book?" Like very cool and sophisticated.

"You know!" said Twink. "The one you were on the cover of... the one about the fat girl."

Oh! I was so hoping they wouldn't have seen it. But I might have known they would. I had to pretend not to care. I mean, there is such a thing as pride. (I may have said this before.) I gushed, "That photo was just so *awful*. They padded it out!"

"They what?" said Zoë.

"Padded it! You know, like they take away people's lines and wrinkles and double chins? They padded it out to make me look fat."

"How do they do that?" said Mitch.

I said, "I don't know *how* they do it, but that's what they did. And it looked so horrible!"

"I thought it looked like you," said Twinkle.

"Oh, thank you very much!" I said.

"So is that when you started slimming?" said Connie.

"I didn't!" I said. "It just happened!"

Saffy made this noise in the back of her throat. There was a pause.

"Well, anyway," said Portia, "you look fab in that gear!"

"If you could just manage to lose another few kilos," said Mitch, "you'd almost l—"

"*Don't!*" That was Saffy, suddenly coming to life. "Just stop encouraging her! She's lost as much as she needs to."

I wondered what Saffy's problem was. Could she be jealous? She'd always been the thin one! I'd been the fat one. Maybe she didn't like me being thin? How utterly pathetic!

I decided yet again that I would take no notice of Saffy. We were having a party to celebrate the end of term – and the end of filming – and I was going to enjoy myself! I went marching out of the changing room with Connie and Portia, leaving Saffy on her own. I didn't think I liked her any more. She was jealous and mean and spiteful! She was trying to ruin my little moment of success. Just because she had gone and forgotten her lines!

The party was totally brilliant, in spite of Saffy skulking around like a big black cloud. I refused to let her spoil things. She was being mean as could be, and I wondered why I'd ever become friends with her.

As soon as we'd changed we all sat down to watch the video. I sat in the middle of the front row, next to Gareth! Saffy sat way back, where in my opinion she belonged. After all, she was little more than a glorified extra. She'd never bothered to develop her part. She'd never become a real character; just someone who occasionally spoke in a (very bad) American accent, saying things which she fondly believed to be American, such as "Gee" and "Shucks" and "Hot damn!" If she hadn't turned up, nobody would have missed her. Whereas if I hadn't turned up, we wouldn't have had a proper ending. So I deserved to sit in front, in the middle, next to gorgeous Gareth. It was like I'd earned the right. I wasn't a nobody any more. I was SOMEONE!

The video lasted three-quarters of an hour. The biggest parts were played by Zoë and Twinkle, and Mark and Gareth, but I was the next biggest! If it hadn't been for the cast being listed in alphabetical order, I would definitely have been number 5. It quite annoyed me that simply because of her surname beginning with B, Saffy was number 2. She didn't deserve it!

When we got to the transformation scene I held my breath thinking, "Please don't let me look fat!"

Well! I didn't look *too* fat. Some people might have said I didn't look fat at all, but once you start slimming you set these very high standards for yourself and know that you can't stop until you have shed every single gram of excess weight. I still had a long way to go. But maybe not everyone agreed with me because guess what? They all applauded!

It was Gareth who started it. When I threw off my old lady raincoat he cried, "Way to go!" and burst into loud clapping, and everyone joined in. Except, probably, Saffy. I bet *she* didn't. I bet she just sat there, all sour and scowling. But who cared about her?

For the party we had loads of nibbles. The two students from the art college stayed on and acted as DJs, and we all danced, including Mrs Ambrose. Even though she was old she could still move! It made me realise that when she was young she must have been really good. It made me think about being old, and how horrid it must be; but I only thought about it for a few seconds as Gareth asked me to dance. He danced with me and with Zoë, but not with anyone else. I didn't dance with anyone else, either. It was Gareth or nobody! I knew that Ben would have liked to dance with me. I could see him, out of the corner of my eye, hovering and quivering, but I kept pretending not to notice. If he wanted someone to dance with, he could dance with Saffy. Not me!

It was really difficult to avoid picking at the nibbles as everyone kept getting into little huddles round the table and people would have noticed if I hadn't eaten anything. Plus I didn't want to give that spiteful Saffy any chance to start up. So I picked and nibbled along with everyone else, thinking to myself that I would do my usual thing. Stick my fingers down my throat before I went to bed. I couldn't afford to start putting on weight again!

Mum came at eight o'clock to pick me up.

"How did it go?" she said. "Where's Saffy?"

We usually gave Saffy a lift, because although she lives in the same road it is quite a long walk.

"Where is she?" said Mum. "Isn't she coming with us?"

"I think she's going with someone else," I said.

"Oh. Well! All right." Mum sounded a bit surprised. She is used to me and Saffy going round like we are stuck together with Super Glue. "You're sure you don't want to wait for her?"

"No," I said. "Let's go! Oh, I must just say goodbye to Gareth."

He was standing with Zoë on the front steps. I sidled over and said, "Byee!" Gareth said, "Bye, Jen," and flapped a hand. Zoë looked at me as if I were dog dirt. She said, "See ya, Granny!" Jealous cow. She was as bad as Saffy.

As always on a Saturday, me and Mum, and Pip and Petal, went up to Giorgio's for dinner. I said that I had already eaten hugely at the party, but then Dad came out with a big plate of something creamy and gluggy that he had just invented.

"Pumpkin Pavlova!"

He said that he had made it specially for me, and he sat himself down at the table and insisted that I try some.

"Just a mouthful!"

Dad's mouthfuls are like elephant bites. Eeeenormous!

"Come on," he said. "Open up!"

Everyone in the restaurant was looking, and laughing, and I just didn't know how I could get out of it. I couldn't create a scene in the restaurant! Plus Dad had made it specially. So I reluctantly opened my mouth and let him spoon in the lovely disgusting gooey concoction, and oh, it was so scrummy! Before I knew it I'd let him feed me the whole plateful. Well, Mum tried a bit, but Petal and Pip turned their noses up and Dad knew better than to push them. I was the foodie!

The minute I'd eaten it, the very *minute* I'd eaten it, I felt myself balloon. I actually felt myself getting fat. I could have wept! How could I be so lacking in self-control? So *stupid*? All my hard work, ruined, in one mad moment of gluttony. I wanted to go running off to the loo right there and then, and stick my fingers down my throat, but it is too horrid in Giorgio's loo. I mean, it is quite clean – I *think*. But it is tiny and dark, like a cell. The floor is concrete and the walls are whitewashed, and the thought of kneeling down with my head in a toilet bowl where strangers had done things – ugh! I couldn't. I would have to wait, in my fatness, until I got home.

But then we stayed late at the restaurant because some people came in that Mum knew and they sat down at the table next to us and Mum started talking, and then Giorgio came over and *he* started talking, and by the time we arrived home I was just so tired!

Once I could have stayed up all night, practically, but these days I was almost never awake when Dad got back from work. I even, sometimes, felt myself falling asleep at school. And not just in maths classes! I'd even nodded off in the middle of English, while we were reading *Jane Eyre*.

There are those who might say that *Jane Eyre* is quite a boring book, being so long and so old-fashioned, but I don't think so. I was enjoying it! I hadn't wanted to go to sleep; it was just this thing that happened. It kept happening. It happened that night, when we got back from Giorgio's.

I thought, I'll just get undressed and lie down for a bit, and wait till Mum's watching telly, then I would go to the loo and offload all the foul fattening food that I had shovelled into myself. Instead, I fell asleep! When I woke up next morning, it was too late. The foul fattening food had all been digested and gone into my system. I heaved and heaved, but nothing came. And then Petal banged on the door and yelled, "What are you doing in there? I'm bursting!" and I had to give up.

I managed not to eat any breakfast, because Mum and Dad were having their Sunday morning lie-in, and Petal was getting ready to go somewhere, and I thought that Pip wouldn't notice if I shrank to a shadow. He probably wouldn't notice if we all shrank to shadows. The only thing he would notice would be if his computer blew up.

After not eating breakfast I scooted upstairs to the bathroom to weigh myself. *Disaster! Of cosmic proportions.* I had put on half a kilo! It depressed me so much I nearly went straight back downstairs to raid the fridge. I just managed to stop myself in time. I made this vow that I would starve for the whole of the rest of the week. I had to be strong-minded!

It is actually very boring, starving yourself. It is all right while you are obsessed, as every meal you don't eat is like a big victory. You feel all the fat dropping off and it gives you a tremendous sense of achievement. But you only need one little setback, like eating nibbles at the party, all those crisps and sausage rolls, and then gorging on Dad's new creation, and instead of being obsessed and triumphant you are simply struggling, every minute of the day, to resist the temptation of FOOD. All the joy goes out of life. Instead of looking forward (like normal people) to meal times and wondering what goodies you will eat, or gloating (like obsessive dieting people) over all the goodies you are *not* going to eat, you are just left with this grey boredom and mental torment. It is no fun at all. It is miserable!

To make matters worse, Saffy and me didn't seem to be on speaking terms. It was the last week of term, so school was quite relaxed. Normally, we would have enjoyed ourselves, but we were just too busy trying never to be in the same space. If Saffy sat at the back of the class, I would sit at the front. If she went out at breaktime, I would stay in. All week long we managed to avoid each other, but then on Friday we had this terrific bust-up. We were going out through the school gates.

I was on my own: Saffy was on her own. We had to walk up the same bit of road to the same bus stop and catch the same bus. Before I could stop myself I had blurted out, "Look, what exactly is your problem?"

Saffy tossed her head and said, "I don't have any

problem! You're the one with the problem. Going round starving yourself!"

"I happen to be on a *diet*," I said.

"Call that a diet?" said Saffy. "More like a death wish!"

I told her that she was obviously jealous, because of me being one of the stars of *Sob Story* and her going and forgetting her lines. Not that I actually said the word "star"; that would have been too vulgar. Too like Zoë. I think what I probably said was "one of the leads". I can't be sure, because at the time I was just so monstrously angry. Saffy was angry, too. She told me that I had become totally self-obsessed.

"All you ever think about is *you*." And then she said that I had made a complete idiot of myself at the party on Saturday. "Smooching up to Gareth like that! Going all goo-goo eyed. It was pathetic!"

I said, "I knew you were jealous!"

"Jealous of what?" screeched Saffy. All shrill and squeaky. She'd never done anything about her voice.

"Jealous of me and Gareth," I said.

Saffy made a scoffing noise. She said, "What's to be jealous of?"

"Because he danced with me," I said.

"Oh! Big deal," said Saffy. "Why should I care if he danced with you?"

I said, "Because he's one of the coolest boys there and *everyone* would like to dance with him!"

"Who says?" said Saffy.

"Well, if you'd rather dance with old Turnip Head," I said. "It seems a bit odd, considering you were the one that said we were going to drama school specially to meet gorgeous guys and the only one you can get is a turnip head!"

Saffy turned bright scarlet. She said, "Ever since you started on this stupid weight thing you've got meaner and meaner! You were really mean to poor Ben the other day. You really upset him!"

I said, "When did I upset him?"

"When he wanted you to be his partner and you wouldn't!"

I said, "No, because I wanted to do my own thing!"

"You wanted to show off," said Saffy crushingly. "And you just made yourself look stupid anyway. Utterly *pathetic*!"

We quarrelled all the way to the bus stop. We quarrelled while we waited for the bus. When the bus came, I went inside, Saffy went on top. When Saffy got out, four stops later, she didn't even look at me. She'd already told me, "I never want to speak to you again!" To which I had retorted, "Just as well, 'cos I don't want to speak to you!"

We had been best friends since the age of six. Now we hated each other.

These things happen.

ten

Now it's Friday evening. I'm up in my bedroom, having a fit of the glooms. I've quarrelled with Saffy and I'm utterly, totally depressed. I shouldn't be. I've lost all that weight and I've been a success and I've danced with gorgeous Gareth. But I am! I am just so-o-o depressed.

I haven't only quarrelled with Saffy, I've quarrelled with Mum and Dad as well. Quarrelling with Mum is not that unusual, but quarrelling with Dad is practically unheard of. Dad just isn't a quarrelling kind of person.

It was this afternoon when I quarrelled with Mum. I got home early from school (because of breaking up) to find that Mum was already here. Surprise, surprise!

When is Mum ever at home when I get back from school? I made the mistake of saying so. I said, "Surprise, surprise! Has the bottom dropped out of the housing market?"

I thought that was quite clever, actually. It was meant to be *funny*, but I think it must have come out as a bit – well, sarcastic maybe. I was still seething about Saffy and was just in this really vile mood.

Mum snapped, "I can do without that tone of voice, thank you very much!" I guess she was in a bit of a mood, too. She'd raced back home, all in a lather, to pick up some papers she needed. She said, "Some of us round here have appointments to keep!" pushing rudely past me as she did so. I said, "Well, gosh, don't let me stop you."

"Jenny, I'm warning you," said Mum. She paused at the door to point a threatening finger at me. "I've had just about enough of you recently. You'd better mend your manners, my girl, or you'll find yourself in trouble!"

With that she was gone, leaving me standing there, speechless. What had I done to deserve such treatment? Dad then came bowling in, wanting to know what was going on.

"Who's having a go at who?"

I said, "*She* is."

"She?" said Dad. "Are you referring to your mother?"

"Oh!" I said. "Is that who it was? I thought it was some stranger come into the house!"

"What exactly do you mean by that?" said Dad.

"That woman that was yelling at me," I said. *"My mother.* I didn't recognise her! Does she live here?"

Well! That was when Dad blew up. Unlike most chefs, who are extremely temperamental and will run at you with murder in their hearts and a carving knife in their hands on the least provocation, Dad is really a very amiable, easygoing person. But there is one thing he will not tolerate, and that is any criticism of Mum. He told me how Mum had worked her fingers to the bone, providing for us all, and said if I couldn't keep a civil tongue in my head I could go to my room. So I came up here and have been here ever since.

It's now six o'clock and Dad has gone off to work. Mum isn't yet back, Petal (I think) is in her room, Pip (I think) is in his room. I, of course, am in my room. Brooding and resentful. Why does everything always, *always* seem to go wrong for me? Why can't I be like Petal and Pip? Nothing ever goes wrong for them. Petal is beautiful, Petal is slim: Petal is popular, Petal has boyfriends. Pip is a genius; Mum spoils him. He's her favourite, without any doubt.

I am consumed with self-pity, and with vengeful envy of them both. My sister and my little brother. I think that Petal is probably slapping on the lip gloss, getting ready to go out with her latest gorge male, while the boy genius will be on his computer, lost somewhere out in cyberspace, doing whatever it is that techno freaks do. Not a cloud on either of their horizons!

I decide to go to the bathroom and weigh myself. I haven't done it for at least an hour. As I open my bedroom door I hear the sound of weeping. It's Petal! She's crumpled in a heap at the top of the stairs, dramatically  clutching her mobile phone to her bosom and sobbing her heart out. I cry, "Petal! What's wrong?" I drop to my knees beside her and she raises a tear-stained face and wails, "My life is over!"

I say, "Why? What's happened?"

She sobs that it's Andy (her latest gorge male). "He's going with another girl!"

I feel like pointing out that Andy is not the only gorge male in the world, that he is not the first gorge male she has been out with (I should think he must be at least number 3, or even 4) and that with her looks she can pick up another one "just like that!" But I don't, because I realise that at this moment in time it will be of no comfort. There can never be another male as gorge as Andy. If he has deserted Petal for someone else, then that is it. THE END. Life has nothing more to offer. All I can do is commiserate.

"Oh, Petal," I go, "I'm so sorry!"

Petal immediately bursts into renewed sobbing and begins to rock to and fro. While she is rocking, the door of Pip's bedroom is thrown open and Pip rushes out. He doesn't even look at me and Petal. He dives into the bathroom, and I hear a crash as the door of the bathroom cabinet flies back and bounces off the bathroom wall. Pip then reappears, with something in his hand. It looks like a bottle of aspirin. It *is* a bottle of aspirin!

"Pip," I say, "what are you doing?"

He looks at me, wild-eyed. He says that he is going to put himself out of his misery. He has tried smothering himself with a pillow, and now he is going to swallow aspirin.

"Go away, Pumpkin!" He pushes me to one side and makes a dive for his bedroom. "You can't stop me!"

But I can. I do! I grab hold of him and scream, "Are you out of your mind?"

Pip says no, he's not out of his mind, he's a *failure*. He is no longer top of his class. He has come second. *Second!* Shock, horror! The shame of it is more than he can bear. He is going to take aspirin and put an end to it all.

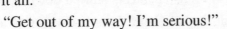

"Get out of my way! I'm serious!"

I'm serious, too. I can't believe it! A ten-year-old boy, wanting to put an end to it all? This is madness! Are we all neurotic wrecks in this family?

By now, Petal has come to her senses and taken note of what's happening. Between us, we march Pip into his bedroom and sit him down on his bed, one of us on either side. Sternly, Petal says, "What is this all about?"

Pip says again that he has lost first place (to a boy called Fur Ball Donnegan, or at least that is what it sounds like) and that his life is at an end. I say, "That makes three of us."

"You as well?" cries Petal. "What's your problem?"

What *is* my problem? I think about it. It's not just that I've fallen out with my best friend and got into trouble with Mum and Dad. I hate, hate, *hate* quarrelling with Saffy, I'm none too keen on having Mum get mad at me, and it's perfectly horrid to have upset Dad; but those are only symptoms. The real problem is that *I am not happy*.

I wonder to myself, was I happy before? When I was fat? A happy fatty! I think that on the whole I was. I was happy in my fatness! I wasn't happy in my thinness. I spent every waking hour worrying about food and whether I was eating too much. My life had become bounded by food! My stomach kept rumbling, I was permanently starving. I weighed myself up to a dozen times a day. My throat was sore from having fingers stuffed down it. My ribs ached from all the heaving I'd done. I was tired and cross and crotchety. I was *miserable*. But I did so want to be thin! I wanted to have cheekbones. And hip bones, and thigh bones, and just *bones*, generally.

160

Petal, meanwhile, is still waiting for an answer to her question: what is my problem? I give a deep sigh and say, "I thought being thin would make me happy!"

"Ye-e-e-es..." Petal considers me, her head to one side. "You *are* thin! You've lost weight!"

"That's because she hasn't been eating," said Pip.

What??? That shakes me! I wouldn't have thought he'd notice. Can it be that Pip sees more than we realise?

"When she does eat," he tells Petal, "she goes and sicks it up again. She's got that bullimer thing."

"That what?" says Petal.

"He means bulimia," I say. "Like Princess Di. It's what she had. But I haven't! I only sick up when I've been on a binge."

"That's what people do when they've got bullimer," says Pip.

How does he know???

"Pump, this is terrible!" cries Petal. "You could die!"

"Let's all die together," says Pip.

Petal rounds on him. Her tears, miraculously, have quite disappeared.

"We'll do no such thing!" she tells Pip. "Give me those aspirin!" She snatches them from him. "What's the matter with this family?"

In tones of morbid satisfaction I say, "We're dysfunctional."

"Well, it's got to stop," says Petal. "If Mum and Dad aren't around to keep an eye on us we'll just have to keep an eye on ourselves. In future, we'll all watch out for one another!"

And for starters she reads Pip this long lecture about exams not being the be-all and end-all, and how coming second in a class of twenty-two is hardly what any sane person would consider a disaster.

"Most people would think they'd done *well*!"

She says that Pip has had too many pressures put on him.

"The family isn't going to collapse if you only come second instead of top! You've got to stop trying to be a genius all the time and start behaving like a normal boy!"

Then she gets going on me. "From now on you are going to eat *properly*. Do you understand? You are not going to go on binges and then sick up. You are not going to go on binges *full stop*. When Dad pushes stuff at you, you just say *no*."

I wail that this is easier said than done. "He gets so upset!"

"So he gets upset! So what? It's better than you having *bulimia*!"

I admit that it is, but am doubtful whether I will have sufficient willpower to resist the temptation. Petal assures me that either she or Pip will always be there to watch over me. I say, "But you can't *always* be there!"

"We can for the holidays," said Petal. "By the time we go back to school you'll have developed all new habits and will be safe to be left on your own."

She gives me her promise. So does Pip. I begin to feel a bit more optimistic. I almost begin to feel *happy*. It is good to have a brother and sister to look after you! I tell Pip that in return me and Petal will help him behave more like a normal ten year old and less like a poor little boy genius with the weight of the world on his shoulders. And then I say, "But what about you?" looking rather hard at Petal.

Petal says I don't have to worry about her.

"I'll be so busy watching out for you and Pip I won't have time to think about myself. In any case," she adds, "I'm through with boys."

Whatever! She needn't think I believe *that*. Not for one moment!

When Mum gets home, about an hour later, we're all sitting in a row on the sofa, watching telly. A thing we

never do! Not all in a row. But it's like we suddenly have this need to stay close. Mum is in one of her brisk moods. I mean, brisker-even-than-usual moods. She cries, "Come on, you lot! Have you eaten? Let's go up the road, I can't be bothered to cook."

When does she ever? Cook, I mean.

"Well, come on!" Mum snaps off the television. She doesn't bother asking us what we're watching, or whether we want to go on watching. We probably don't – I'm not even sure we know what channel we're on. But that is Mum for you.

She hustles us out of the house. I exchange nervous glances with Petal. Well, my glance is nervous; Petal's is reassuring. She clamps her arm through mine and hisses, "Stand firm. We're with you!"

One of the waiters, Angelo (who is rather divine and has a bit of a thing about Petal) shows us to our usual table, the big round one in the corner. He then rushes off to the kitchen, where we hear him calling out to Dad.

"Eh! Franco!" (Dad's name in Italian.) "Your *famiglia* is here!"

Dad bustles out to see us, in his chef's apron and hat. Beaming, he says that he has just prepared some fresh pasta. One of his specials. I gulp. I adore Dad's pastas! Petal squeezes my hand.

"We'll just have salads," she says.

"What?" Dad looks from me to Petal in bewilderment. Obviously can't believe he's heard right. "Pumpkin's not having salad!"

"She is," says Petal. "We both are."

"Rubbish!" says Dad. "You can eat like a rabbit if you want. I'm not having Pumpkin infected by the bug!"

Earnestly, I say that it's not a bug. "It's healthy eating!"

It's a bit of a feeble protest, but I can't leave it all to Petal. Pip obviously feels the same, because he pipes up in support.

"Give us salad! We want salad!" And then he adds, "*Green*."

"Green for him, mixed for us," says Petal.

Poor Dad is looking more and more confused. Even Mum seems to realise that something isn't quite as it should be. Little Podgy Plumpkin eating *salad*? Since when?

"Now, look," says Dad, "this is ridiculous! You can't just eat a few lettuce leaves, young lady. You'll have a nice plate of pasta, with salad on the side. Right?" And he turns away, as if the matter is now settled. Which, if it had been me on my own, with Petal making eyes at the waiters and Pip solving puzzles in his head, it probably would have been. I would never find the strength to hold out against Dad! But Petal has a lot of what I would call *backbone*. She definitely has a stubborn streak. Luckily for me!

"Dad," she says, "we're having salads. We don't want pasta."

Mum suddenly wakes up and rushes in to Dad's support. "Pasta's good for you!"

"Now and again," says Petal. "Not every day. Not in the quantities Dad dishes it up!"

"Not with that horrid red sauce," says Pip. "Ugh! *Glug*."

Not really very helpful, but at least he is trying.

"Maybe tomorrow," says Petal. "Tomorrow she can have pasta... but just a *small* helping."

Oh, dear! It is so embarrassing. I feel that everyone in the restaurant is watching us, waiting to see what will happen.

Somewhat crossly, Mum says to Petal, "You've become very bossy all of a sudden!"

"One of us has to be," says Petal.

Dad now decides that the time has come to make a stand.

"See here," he says, "I won't have you bullying your sister! You keep your food fads to yourself. Plumpkin's got more sense. She's a foodie, aren't you, poppet? Same as her dad!"

"Not any more," says Petal.

"No!" Pip bangs triumphantly on the table with the salt cellar. "Not any more! This is the start of a new regime!" He uses words like that. I suppose it's what comes of being a boy genius. "We're in charge now!"

"That's *right*," says Petal. "We've taken over."

"Taken over what?" says Mum.

"Well, Pump's intake, for one thing," says Petal. "We're monitoring it."

"What for?" Mum now seems every bit as bewildered as Dad. "She's not fat! In fact—" She narrows her eyes, studying me across the table. It's like she's seeing me for the first time. I want to dive beneath the red check tablecloth and hide. I feel like some kind of exhibit. "Have you lost weight?" says Mum.

Petal rolls her eyes. I mean, she hadn't noticed either, until today, but then she is only my sister. Pip, growing excited, bangs again with the salt cellar and cries, "Hooray! Mum gets a gold star!"

By now, you can see that both Mum and Dad are

completely at a loss. They haven't the faintest idea what's going on! Petal, taking pity on them, says kindly that there's no need for them to worry.

"Just leave it to us. We're quite capable of looking after ourselves."

There's a silence; then Dad shakes his head, as if it's all just got too much, and goes trundling back to the kitchen to prepare one plate of pasta and three salads. Poor Dad! He can't work out what's hit him.

"There you are," says Petal. She nods at me, and pats my hand. "That was quite painless, wasn't it?"

Pip yells, "Kids unite!" and beats a tattoo with his knife and fork. Almost like a normal ten year old! Maybe there is hope for us all.

Mum is still studying me with this puzzled expression on her face, like she's trying to decide whether I've always looked like I do now, or whether her eyes are deceiving her.

"I hope you're not getting anorexic," she says.

"Mum, she is not getting anorexic," says Petal. "She *might* have been – but we've put a stop to it. Now she's going to eat sensibly. Aren't you?"

I nod, meekly.

"We're going to help her," says Petal.

Mum says, "But—" And then she stops, puts both hands on top of her head and closes her eyes. "All right," she says. "We're obviously going to have to talk."

"We can," says Petal, "if you like. There are certainly things to talk about."

"That," says Mum, "is becoming painfully clear."

Poor Mum! I've never seen her so... chastened, I think, is the word. Like when someone tells you off and you know that you've deserved it. Not that anyone has told Mum off! But she seems to be having guilt feelings, as if maybe she hasn't been a proper mum. I feel like telling her that it's not her fault. I like having a mum who's a high flyer! I'm proud of her! She can't be expected to go out every day doing an important job like hers *and* take notice of all the little banal things going on around her. How was she to know I wasn't eating properly? Or that Petal was tearing herself to pieces over ratlike Andy, and Pip wearing his brain to a frazzle?

Petal, kindly, says, "Don't worry! It'll all get sorted out."

Mum just gives her this look. The sort of look I imagine a plant might give before you brutally wrench it out of the earth.

"I don't know," she says, wearily. "I just don't know!"

It's Dad who brings out our salads. (Angelo's standing at the kitchen door, grinning.) Being Dad, of course, he can't just do plain *salad*. On mine and Petal's he's added new potatoes, hard-boiled eggs, slices of salami (on mine, not Petal's) and a sprinkling of parmesan. Humbly he asks if that is all right.

"Everything except the salami," says Petal. "She can't have that."

Dad opens his mouth to protest, but Petal cuts firmly over the top of him.

"You don't want to eat *animal*," she says. "Do you?"

I don't particularly want to eat animals; but I do like salami!

"*Do* you?" says Petal.

I go, "W—"

"Apart from anything else," says my remorseless sister, "such as for instance being disgusting and cruel and utterly repulsive, it is *chock full of fat*."

Pip goes, "Ugh!"

"Yes. Ugh!" says Petal.

Very meekly, Dad removes the salami from my plate and puts it into his mouth. Someone in the restaurant starts a round of applause. Angelo, over by the kitchen door, thrusts a clenched fist into the air. We watch, as Dad chews and swallows.

"Is that better?" he says.

"Yes! Thank you." Petal gives him one of her dazzling smiles (the ones she uses to get gorge males). "That is *healthy*!"

In weak tones, quite unlike her normal up-front self, Mum says, "Why do I get the feeling we're being ganged up against?"

"Because you are!" squeals Pip. "We're the Gang of Three and we are **YEW**nited!"

It's funny, we've never been that close, the three of us. We've all tended to do our own thing, go our separate ways. Now, suddenly, we're like a proper family. We're all going to pull together! It makes me feel warm and safe. I'm so glad I have a brother and sister! I haven't always been. There have been times when I would cheerfully have drowned them both in buckets of water. I expect there may be more times like that in the future. But just right now, I love them both to bits!

finale

WELL, I SUPPOSE really that I have reached the end, at least of this particular bit of my life. My struggle with fat!

The struggle goes on, except that I am not obsessed any more. I am trying very hard to *eat sensibly*. I am determined not to go back to being the human equivalent of a dustbin, and even Dad is beginning to accept that he cannot pile up my plate the way he used to.

We had this long, long talk, Mum and Dad, me and Petal and Pip. Mum said, "I have been such a bad mother!" Dad said, "No, I have!" which made us laugh. Mum then said, in all seriousness, that perhaps she should give up her job; at which we all shouted, "Mum! *No!*" Dad said maybe he should be the one to give up, but Mum said that wouldn't be fair. She said he'd already done his stint as a househusband. In the end we unanimously decided to continue just as we were, except that from now on we were all going to sit down, once a week, as a family, and *share*.

I must say that it has worked quite well. We all gather round the table and say what we've been doing. We "air our grievances" and ask if anyone has got any problems they want to discuss. We tell all the good things that have happened, and the bad things, too. I know more about Mum and Dad, and about Pip and Petal, than I ever did before!

Pip still works really hard, but I think, now, it's because he likes to rather than because he's under pressure. Petal still obsesses over boys; I can't see that ever changing! But just recently she seems to have settled down a bit. She's been going with the same one for almost three months, which is practically a record! I expect sooner or later they will break up, and then we shall have tears, and marathon wailing sessions on her mobile, but at least she will be able to tell us about it and we can all sympathise.

As for me... it has not been easy, learning to eat properly. But everyone has helped, and I think that I can *almost* trust myself. I fear that I shall never be thin as a pin; I just don't seem to be made that way. I am doing my best to be happy with my body, because after all it is the only one I am ever likely to have. Not that it stops me yearning! I would still rather be slim, slender and stick-like than pudgy, podgy and plump. I would think almost anyone would. I don't care what people say! But you can't always be how you would like to be, and I have come to the conclusion that there is simply no point in making yourself miserable over it.

I once read that inside every fat person there is a thin person waiting to get out. But the way I see it, inside every short person there is probably a tall person. And everyone with thin hair would probably die to have thick hair. And those with long droopy faces would just love to have round cheeky faces. And those that are plain would give anything to be beautiful. But that is the way it goes.

As I said at the beginning, dream on!

Actually, I don't think I did say it, but I could have done. I could have said a lot of things, only it is a bit late now. I have told my story and it is time to finish.

Oh, I made up with Saffy, by the way. I couldn't stand not being friends with her! She said that she couldn't stand not being friends with me. I apologised for being so mean and cranky, Saffy apologised for not being more understanding. Now we are closer than ever!

We still go to drama classes because we really do enjoy them. We are working on a musical this term. I have discovered that I can sing! We are still in search of those hunky, sensitive boys... we still live in hope, though Mark has left to go to a full-time drama school in London and gorgeous Gareth has moved away. Boo hoo! Little Miss Twinkle and Zoë are still with us. *Unfortunately*. But they don't bug me any more, even though Zoë has taken to calling me Heffelump. I have learnt to ignore her. I just rise above it! A couple of new boys have started taking classes, and we think, me and Saffy, that they may turn out to be quite promising...

but actually, at the moment, I am sort of going out with Ben. He may look like a turnip, but he makes me laugh! We have lots of fun together.

I have decided, however, that I don't want a career in the movies after all. I don't think I am really cut out for it; I am not show-offy enough. What I am considering at the moment is entering one of the *caring* professions. Helping people. Saving the rainforests. That sort of thing. I think it is ignoble to just aim for fame or money. Of course, I may change my mind about this. I have changed it several times in the past! But those are my feelings at this moment in time.

Oh, and hey! Guess what? They have done another *Ellen* book and I am on the cover again! I'm dead proud of it. As soon as it hits the shops I'm going to be out there, making sure it can be seen. If that author doesn't end up rich as rich can be, it certainly won't be my fault!